Virginia Betts is a British author and tutor born in Ipswich, Suffolk, in 1971. She graduated from Essex University with a BA in Literature and Sociology in 1994, then completed a post-graduate degree in teaching. She taught for 15 years before forming her tuition company, Results Tutoring, in 2013, where she indulges her love of literary analysis whilst helping her students. She has a particular gift for working with the neurodiverse, being neurodiverse herself, and has been featured in *Your Autism* magazine as an advocate for the *National Autistic Society*. Her first published work was a short story, *The Rented Room,* (*The Weird and Whatnot July 2019*), and a poem, *An Afternoon Walk*, (*Acumen, September 2019).* Since then, she has had stories, poetry, non-fiction articles and memoirs published in literary journals, anthologies and magazines both online and in print. She is a regular speaker and reader on BBC Radio, and has written for and acted in professional theatre, working with *The Wolsey Writers, The Wolsey Theatre, The Neurodelicious Launch Pad, Suffolk Writers Group, The Suffolk Poetry Society* and *Hightide Theatre Company.* She is currently working on a second book of stories and a novel, *Arianne.* Virginia's poetry collection, *Tourist to the Sun,* will be also published shortly. Virginia is married with one son, and apart from her work, enjoys swimming and playing the violin.

For my parents, Christine and John Runnacles and Eric Blomfield, 'Gug', for everything, always; for my husband, Kevin, for being my best friend forever; for my son, Jacob Rush – live your dreams.

Also, to Tim Howard – an inspirational teacher.

And finally, dedicated to Joan Sylvia Cecelia Blomfield, a truly great storyteller.

Virginia Betts

THE CAMERA OBSCURE

AUSTIN MACAULEY PUBLISHERS™

LONDON • CAMBRIDGE • NEW YORK • SHARJAH

A CIP catalogue record for this title is available from the British Library.

ISBN 9781398423510 (Paperback)
ISBN 9781398423527 (ePub e-book)

www.austinmacauley.com

First Published 2022
Austin Macauley Publishers Ltd®
1 Canada Square
Canary Wharf
London
E14 5AA

The Rented Room

It is commonly understood that along with a birth, a death, and a divorce, moving house is one of life's most stressful events. I had no close, personal experience of the first three but I was ready to risk the last, as the time had come to move on. Feeling the familiar impulse to start looking over my shoulder once again, I sold my place of solitary refuge and was about to flee to the other end of the country. A writer, always hoping to add one more chapter to my own tale, it was entirely fitting that I was here, almost ready to leave, boxing up my treasured books.

As I picked up the last dust-covered book and placed it carefully into the box, I found myself considering that night so long ago. I sat surrounded by cardboard vessels filled with printed tales to delight and horrify, but of all the stories I have written and read, none made such an indelible mark on my life as the story I became a part of some 40 years ago. It seemed like only days back that the terrible events unfolded around me, although a lifetime had withered and died in those same hours and minutes.

No, I was not the same person who had embarked on my journey all those years previously. The mirror that once reflected a face full of hope and promise, now framed a weary, ageing visage with eyes clouded by fear and defeat. I checked the book I had just placed into the box, almost as if it would reveal a secret to me or point me to a destiny I had yet to reach. It was a collection of poetry by Philip Larkin. I knew the poems it contained. One of them, *Mr Bleaney,* beginning 'This was Mr Bleaney's room', reminded me of the landlady's words to me when I'd had arrived in Paradise Street on that fateful day, 40 years ago.

It had been an uneventful journey to reach my destination that day. I had taken the train in the morning and then found myself, by means of a newly purchased map, rounding the corner into Paradise Street, the location housing the address I sought. The street was ordinary enough; perhaps it was a little narrow but otherwise a quiet and orderly area. I strode with a spring in my step. Newly qualified as a schoolteacher and having commenced writing my first novel with an advance from a publisher, I felt that life offered me a wealth of treasures to uncover and even the wintry wind at my collar did not unduly irk me. The map flapped in the wind as I tried to check my location was correct and, as I did so, I skidded on a patch of hidden ice.

"Bugger!" I exclaimed, hurriedly looking around to check that no one had spotted my ignominious slide. I regained my composure, glad I had not fallen to the wet ground, and stopped walking. I looked up and down the long street. I smiled at the irony of the street name, 'Paradise.' This was a far from accurate description. It was simply an ordinary street, containing the usual rows of houses and shops, some cheerful and some dreary, all hunched up together as if comforting each other against the cold. One building, however, stood out from the rest. It looked as if it belonged to another time and seemed to assert its own individual character on the street. It was a shopfront with a classical-style protruding glass window, divided into small panes. The mullions, sill, cornices, and fascia were all painted in maroon and the display inside showcased rows and rows of books, of eclectic style and genre, almost beckoning the customer inside. Despite the wintry sun, the interior looked old and dark, yet the books gave the shop colour and vibrancy and I was intrigued. I checked the map for my location as I knew the address I sought was in this street. I checked the address again. It seemed that the address of the flat I planned to view that day was right here in this bookshop.

There was no one in sight to ask and as the weather was so cold, I decided that my best chance was to go inside the bookshop and see if there was anyone who could shed some light on the situation. I peered at the sign above the door. In large gold-leaf letters it read, 'Eden Books'. Underneath, in smaller lettering, it read, 'Proprietor, Mr Carstairs Nile, Esq.'. I tried the door and it swung open easily, caught by the wind, and precipitating the jingle of the bell above the door to alert the assistant to customers.

"Excuse me," I said, timidly, "is there anyone around who can help me? I'm supposed to look at a flat here but the address seems to match this bookshop."

A flustered-looking woman, middle-aged and shabbily dressed, came hurrying into the shop. "Are you Mr Fairfax?" she inquired. "Because you have got the right place, it's just that there is a side door leading into the flats and it's hidden from the street if you don't know the area. I must have forgotten to mention it. Do come through. I'm Janet Underworth, the landlady, technically. I live in the flat at the back and the one you're after is upstairs." She made a fast, beckoning motion and had already started to walk away. "Come through, I've got the keys and full approval to show you around."

I paused. "Who is Mr Nile then? Does he own the bookshop?"

"To be honest, not many people ever get to meet Mr Carstairs in person. Oh, sorry, I mean Mr Nile. I always call him Mr Carstairs, on account of mistaking his Christian name for his surname when I first met him. It sort of stuck." She paused, as if aware of talking too much, but continuing anyway. "So, he owns the bookshop, yes, and also the flats really but because he is always travelling so much, picking up new stock and so forth, I keep the place for him and act as Landlady. I work in the shop, look after the tenant upstairs and make sure all his affairs here are in order. He's not a marrying type, so, as you can imagine, the place needs a woman to keep things ticking over. Come on then!" She beckoned for me to cross the threshold properly and go after her.

I followed her through the bookshop, weaving my way between the dusty shelves and dangling oriental lampshades. I was an avid reader, naturally, given my dual professions, and I had literally hundreds of books of all types and subjects. But this bookshop seemed stocked to the brim with tomes I would be happy to spend hours poring over. There was hardly room to pass between the shelving and as I negotiated them, somehow one or two of them fell despite my care, and I stooped to replace them. The dusty and leathery aroma filled my nostrils and I reflected that like the name of the street, this to me was paradise, of a sort.

Ever since I was a child, it was almost a foregone conclusion that I would be destined to become either a writer or a keeper of books. I had been obsessed with them, devouring their contents as soon as I could read, being transported to other worlds and far off lands in my head. I qualified as a teacher to ensure that I had a sensible career with which to provide myself and a future family an income but I had chosen English because I felt I could also imbue other young minds with the same love of literature. I found my first job in this small and insignificant town and had come to find a place to live before the start of term, as the summer shifted into autumn, and the days brought with them an unexpected, premature cold snap.

"This was Mr Hogarth's room," said the landlady, "he stayed here the whole time he worked in the town until they took him away."

"Was that a long time then?" I enquired.

"Ooh, he came here when the flat was done up new. When I took over as a landlady here and had my flat downstairs, this one wasn't in any fit state to let really. But Mr Hogarth, he was happy to take it and do it up a bit."

I glanced around the flat. I felt as if the room's own mood was overwhelming me. A dour, melancholy spirit, a pulsating, lacklustre sigh seemed to heave from every corner. I breathed in the damp, musty aroma. I noted the faded, frayed curtains, and the lack of care apparent in the rest of the upholstery; a torn sofa, faded nets, moth-eaten bedding piled up. It was in its own way, a relic, exuding a testament to an age of monochrome. The landlady, like the accommodation she had to offer, reeked of the past and seemed to carry with her the room's same taint of neglect. Small clues left around the flat, many such cheap trophies from the same seaside town, a couple of photographs, a few scattered newspaper articles in drawers, revealed that he was not a man who had ever ventured far. However, she seemed entranced by her erstwhile tenant.

"Oh, he stayed here for such a long time," she chattered on, "even" – and here she leaned towards me conspiratorially – "even after he passed. It was more than a week he lay," she spoke in a whisper, reverentially.

I looked again at the frayed curtains, the holes, and the chairs. Even the furniture was decades behind its time; cheap and never chic. Behind the door was a single coat hook. The landlady continued to chatter, her words fading in and out of my consciousness as I surveyed the box-like surroundings.

"Oh, he was such a lovely, helpful man. He took such great care of this place you know. He did wonders for my little patch of land. Course, it really all belongs to Mr Carstairs but he never comes and it's as good as mine."

She drew back the decrepit netting, even as I marvelled at her obliviousness. Daylight broke into the murky gloom in watery shards of sunlight, infiltrating areas that appeared not to have seen the light of day, possibly for decades. Insects retreated like vampires to their coffins, woodlice and stray spiders scurried to the corners and under the floorboards as the day invaded.

I peered at the aforementioned patch of land out the window. The sight that greeted me was not altogether unexpected, given the nature of the room and its caretaker. The 'patio', if it could be called that, was a concrete crazy paving riddled with weeds slyly springing up between the cracks. The 'land' backing onto this overgrown area had long since defied any description connected with the word 'lawn'. Reeds of grass shot skyward, as high as a seven-year-old, and scattered about were yellowing weeds and straw and unknown plants. A rusty watering can squatted dryly in one corner and a brown-handled rake in another. I looked from room to land and back again, and the two scenes became almost interchangeable in my mind. Despite this, I turned to the landlady and spoke.

"Well," I said, "your previous guest did stay here a long time, he obviously felt at home, so…I'll take it."

I was soon settled in, having moved as many of my things as I could up in suitcases hauled on and off the train and trundled through the streets. The rest I arranged to be delivered by road transport. Now, a fortnight later, I was still unpacking but the neglected room that wore such a melancholy air began to come to life. It still bore the terrible décor and murky appearance that it inherited from its predecessor but I stamped some of my own personal taste on the room and crucially, I now had my books about me.

I started the term, met my classes with the well-prepared eagerness of a new member of staff and found it to be rewarding, if exhausting, work. I was sometimes disappointed that others did not think in the same way and that my young charges in the days of my training seemed more interested in trivia, sport, and dating than the works of Dickens and Shakespeare. But there were one or two who had been genuinely interested and had shown promise. I felt I could make a difference. I even had time to continue with my own writing a little, in the happy state that I had plenty of time to fulfil my requirements for that contract as they had already liked the first ten thousand words of the manuscript I had sent.

That Friday evening, I took up my position on the sofa with a glass of whiskey and a book to read, purely for my own leisure. The weekend beckoned and I joyfully remembered that I had made plans to visit the cinema the next night, along with a very pretty and earnest young colleague named Mary Martin. In my mind, I was making the most of what life had to offer me.

As I read, I grew steadily sleepier by the glowing firelight. I was beginning to find it difficult to distinguish between what I was reading on the page and what I knew to be a reality, and I must have dozed off with vivid images of Poe's ghostly tale haunting my dreams. I woke to find the flat in darkness and I could hear a strange, intermittent thudding sound coming from downstairs. I wondered what on earth Miss Underworth could be doing but then I remembered that she was away for the weekend. I jumped up and tried to switch the lamp on but it seemed that the light bulb had blown and I remained disorientated and in blackness. I felt around for my lighter on the old coffee table and knocked an old ashtray, which had evidently belonged to Mr Hogarth, onto the floor. Eventually grasping hold of my lighter, I flicked it with shaking hands. The flame flickered, sputtered, and died. I tried again and this time the eerie orange glow illuminated the area with a tiny light. Shapes wavered and distorted and as I tried to move across the room, I almost dropped the lighter with a start. But what I thought was a phantom was only a glimpse of my own face in the looking glass above the fireplace.

Eventually, I made it to the main light switch but when I flicked it that did not yield any light. I began to feel the first prickles of panic creeping across my skin. I stood still in the darkness, aware of my own breathing becoming faster and shallower, and I had difficulty controlling my racing thoughts while I considered what to do. My eyes were growing accustomed to the blackness, so with the aid of my ailing lighter flame, I slowly began to side-step towards the door to make my way to the top of the stairs in the hall.

The long, narrow corridor beckoned, and I groped my way along it, using the wall as support and guidance. All the time I edged closer to the stairs, the dull thudding sound continued, growing more insistent with every tentative step I took. It seemed to mimic the sound of the footsteps of a slow and heavy beast, first a slide, and then a thud, repeating itself again and again, over and over, never changing pace but growing louder and more menacing as I moved towards it.

Finally, I reached the staircase, felt the bulbous wooden post of the banister and despite the failing flame and the looming shadows cast along the wall and ceiling, I stepped gingerly out. One step, two steps, holding on tightly, all the time the rhythmic thudding growing ever more insistent. At the last step, I missed my footing and dropped my lighter into the blackness with an echoing metallic clang. I breathed in. Time seemed suspended. I dared not move. The thud had stopped.

Breathing heavily and with a pounding heart, I sprinted to where I approximated the hall light to be and flicked it. It was a dim lantern but after the pitch blackness, it seemed to flood the hallway with brilliance. The light showed nothing out of place and I stood for a moment to gather my wits, then made my way through into the bookshop itself, flicking on the dull lanterns as I went, fearing an encounter with I knew not what. My imagination was in riotous overdrive, yet I tried to rationalise my thoughts.

Finally, I came to the last of the shelves in the claustrophobic little area. Before me laid an enormous pile of books, scattered about my feet on the floor, as if they had been pushed from the shelves one by one by the fingers of an invisible force. Now the hackles on my neck began to rise, and a slow chill began to spread up my spine like tiny icy feet were tip-toeing along my back.

For a moment, I felt frozen to the spot but for some unfathomable reason, my first reaction was to bend and pick the books up to place them back on the shelves. As I did so, another fell or, and I had little doubt of this, was pushed, and struck me a blow in the neck. I straightened up and turned sharply; one after another of the books began to fly from their housing, lobbed at my face and head with some force. I no longer wanted to stay and tidy up. I dashed for the back of the shop and rushed up the stairs again, tripping and stumbling over my own feet in my panic and did not pause until I had re-entered my dark flat and slammed the door. Catching my breath, I fumbled for the light switch, forgetting that it had not worked before. I snapped it on and oddly this time, it lit up the room.

Glad to be back in the light, I relaxed a little, although I was still shaken. But my respite was short-lived. As my eyes met with the mirror above the fireplace, it appeared to be steamed up, and in the centre one word stood out, 'LEAVE'.

In the few days that followed, I kept the incident to myself, trying to rationalise what had happened. But I cannot pretend that I wasn't unsettled. The next morning, I returned to the scene of the night's disturbance, thinking about how I might explain the scattered books to Mrs Underworth when she returned. However, the books had been placed back on the shelves. This was even more unnerving and I searched for footprints, signs of a break-in or even the remnants of some ghostly ectoplasm dripping from the shelves. But there were no signs and I began to wonder if I had imagined it all.

No more disturbances occurred for a while and I continued with life, working and developing a nice little relationship with Mary Martin. It was fun at school; snatching odd moments between classes, dodging the curious eyes of the children, making dates to see films and have dinner, 'courting', as they still called it in those days.

One evening, standing at my shaving mirror and preparing to meet Mary in the town, I suddenly felt an icy chill. It was not unusual to feel cold, as winter had seemed to have the country in its icy grip since September with no plans to depart, but this was not caused by the weather. The shiver making my skin crawl was familiar.

I laid down my cut-throat razor but kept it close. I felt the room grow cold and my breath condensed on exhalation. It fell so silent that I could hear my own blood pumping around my body and I was aware of every organ working overtime. I began to hear creaking on the stairs, like the footsteps of someone approaching slowly whilst trying to remain hushed.

I dared not leave the bathroom but I listened as the steps seemed to move across the floor of my flat, even as the room I was in appeared to become enveloped in shadow. The bathroom began to steam up. I moved to pick up the razor blade again but it was not where I had placed it. Suddenly, I felt a sharp, stinging sensation, and watched in horror as two words appeared to be carved into the flesh of my torso, *'GET OUT!'* The world began to spin around me and everything went black.

When I awoke, Mary and Mrs Underworth were standing over me with a cup of tea.

"Don't talk," said Mary, "it's all right."

"Just like poor Mr Hogarth," said Mrs Underworth.

"Ssh!" said Mary and turned to me. "Doctor is on his way."

Later, I found myself in a hospital bed, trying to piece together what had happened.

"So, you can't remember anything?" asked the doctor.

"Not really but I didn't do this." I cringed, indicating my bandaged chest. "I know it sounds ridiculous but it seemed to happen by itself like someone was doing it to me."

The man in the white coat raised his eyebrows. "Someone will be along to speak to you tomorrow," he said, "when you feel better."

"Overworked," was the verdict. "Stressed and too much to do with the new school and the book." Discussions about my 'fragile mental health' and 'repressed grief from childhood leading to depressive tendencies' had taken place, and I was cautiously released with medication. Mary promised to keep an eye on me but I noticed that her affections had cooled a little.

"Mary," I said when she was visiting one evening, "do you believe in ghosts?" I saw her face written all over with scepticism and surprise but I proceeded to explain my experiences. "Also," I went on, "other things have happened now that I think about it. Things I can't explain. Just little things, like things going missing and turning up in the wrong place. And my constant lack of energy. What do you think Mrs Underworth meant by 'just like Mr Hogarth'?"

"I don't know, Jacob but all of those things sound like the stress the doctors talked about. I hope you're not going mad."

"Mary, will you stay with me tonight?" I asked tentatively. "Not like that, I'll sleep in here but I just don't feel entirely safe anymore, and it always seems to happen when Mrs Underworth is away."

"All right," she replied.

It must have been the noise that woke me around two in the morning. This time, I was able to snap the lamp on. I could hear it again, thud…thud…thud. I started to rise to wake Mary but she was already by my side.

"What is that, Jacob?" she whispered in alarm.

"That's the noise I heard before! If we go down with a torch, I bet we will find the books being thrown about again!"

We crept down the passage and descended the stairs. My hand shook as I held the heavy torch, lighting our way into the shop. Sure enough, the books were scattered about. Mary gasped when she saw them. Slowly, I shone the torch along the empty shelves.

Suddenly, I jumped back in fear as a grim face loomed up opposite me. It was a pale, narrow face, with sharp cheekbones, aquiline features, and a high forehead. I cried out in terror!

"Good evening, Sir, Madam. I am so sorry to startle you. I just arrived from overseas. My name is Carstairs Nile."

After that first meeting, Mr Nile stayed for a few weeks. He was charming when he conversed with us, although his tall, imposing figure always made me feel uneasy, intimidated perhaps by his not inconsiderable intellect. He seemed to glide between the bookshelves, sometimes speaking to the customers, who were rare indeed, more often reading or cataloguing his wares. Mostly, I avoided him, he seemed to keep odd hours, seldom did he move outside the shop during daylight, and as I was working again and typing up my manuscript at the weekend, I rarely crossed paths with him or Janet Underworth.

Which was why I was so surprised to see him at my door one winter evening. "Good evening," he said, "I thought I would come introduce myself formally. I am sorry I startled you when I arrived. How are you settling in here? Is Mrs Underworth taking care of you?"

"To be honest, I don't see her very often. I have been so busy, you see, with my work and my book, which I regret to say I am behind with. But do come in."

"Ah. Your predecessor was also a writer. Full of energy. He loved being above the bookshop; he was drawn to it like a moth to a flame." The deep voice lingered over every syllable.

"Was he really? Do tell me more. Mrs Underworth seemed to adore him but from what I can see, from the little trinkets he left around the place, he seems to have been a bit of an old stick-in-the-mud!"

"Ah yes. Well, he never did finish anything properly as time went on. Got somewhat depressed shall we say? Lost all his enthusiasm."

"A shame, maybe?" I replied, warily. "Anyway, would you like a drink, sir?"

"Carstairs, please. No, I won't keep you from your business. But if you need anything, Janet is under strict instructions."

"Thank you, Mr Niles." Somehow, the first-name terms seemed far too informal for such an imposing character. "There is one thing though. Did Hogarth or anyone else for that matter, ever report any disturbances around the place? In the bookshop?"

"Disturbances? No. But Mr Hogarth himself was very disturbed. Killed himself in the end, I'm sorry to say."

"I didn't know that. I am sorry to hear it. Well, thank you for visiting me. Next time, do stay for a drink."

"Good evening to you," he said once again.

I was taken with his formal tone. As with much of the building itself, he seemed to belong to a past age, yet he did not suffer the sense of neglect that I had encountered when I first arrived there. However, about Mr Hogarth, I was intrigued. Maybe there was something of his restless spirit still stalking the flat?

The following day, I went to the library. I did not really know what I expected to find but I scoured relentlessly through all the old newspaper reports on record. Eventually, I came to a small headline detailing the suicide of Mr James Hogarth, a horror writer of small fame locally, who had been found dead in his apartment above Eden Books in Paradise Street. He had cut his wrists with a razor blade. Once a promising writer, he had gradually declined into a mental breakdown, believing that characters from his own stories had come to life and were out to kill him. According to the reports, it seemed that he had given up writing and become reclusive, too afraid to leave the flat, and declining into a form of schizophrenia until his death.

It was certainly intriguing but what really leapt out at me was the manner of his death. A razor blade! My thoughts began to stir in my brain and despite trying to suppress such irrational fantasy, I could not help but wonder.

"So, you think Mr Hogarth is haunting this flat and picking on you because he's jealous of your writing? Oh, come on!" scoffed Mary. "Now I do think you're crazy."

"Mary, think about it. I can't explain what happened, and I am feeling so tired, I feel like I'm diminishing slowly. I can't work properly, I've been off work for ages, I've only just gone back to school and I can't concentrate. It's like he's possessing me or something."

"But there have been no more 'hauntings'? No more bumps in the night?" Her voice oozed scepticism. "Surely your landlady or that owner person, Nile isn't it? Surely they would have noticed it by now? I think we can explain it; you got tired, stressed and ill. You were depressed, moving house and all, the stress got to you, and you had a breakdown."

"But Mary, there was no reason for it, not really."

"Your mother died when you were young and you never got over it properly. That's what they all talked about with you. You're getting better, we just have to keep an eye on you." Mary's business-like manner upset me.

"I got over it! I grieved when I was a child!" I protested. "It's not something within me; it's something outside of me."

But Mary remained unconvinced and not that sympathetic. She left earlier than usual that evening and I felt forlorn. I poured myself a whiskey and stared into the fire.

The whiskey began to be a regular addition to my evenings. Instead of working on my book or preparing schoolwork, I would pour a drink and then another; just enough to send me into a stupor that enabled me to sleep. But I did not sleep soundly. Every night after Mr Nile left again, the noises would begin. The thudding and now whispering, and a feeling of fingers lightly brushing my cheek. I could not distinguish between work and sleep. I heard voices, and the foggy nights seemed to infiltrate my room. Mary had abandoned me; I was a drunk with no ambition in her view. I was failing at my school job and on probation, and I missed the first deadline for my book. I could hardly find the energy to raise my head from my pillow these days. By February, I felt as if I had lost the will to live.

It was in the early hours of a Sunday night that I heard the noises again downstairs and I felt I'd had enough. With a final surge of the energy I had left, I hauled myself out of bed and across the room. I made my way downstairs as quietly as I could, determined in my almost insane state, to find out what it was once and for all.

It all happened so fast, and yet it felt like a warped, slow-motion film. I took a step forward into the back of the shop, and with one swift movement, an horrific, cadaverous face was thrust into mine.

"Get out! Now!" the monster hissed. I realised with horror that this withered, consumptive vision was the face of Mr Hogarth.

I screamed and ran forward. But what confronted me next was far worse. I saw the dark figure of Mr Carstairs Nile hovering above the ground over the prostrate body of an unknown victim, with Mrs Underworth looking on salaciously. Nile appeared to be draining the body, not of blood but in an equally vampiric manner, of energy and life. The body shrank and became empty, almost as if its innards were melting away, leaving only the shell. The predators turned and fixed me with malevolent, red-eyed stares. I had no doubt now that I would be next.

They began to move towards me, and in my sickness and horror, I felt my legs buckle.

"Jacob," breathed Nile, "do not fear it. If you stay, you need not die. I just need your energy to survive, as I have done all this time. It was clever of Mrs Underwood to find you; she has served me all these years, so faithfully, and in return, she lives. I fed on Hogarth and he was able to live but in the end, I needed someone younger, more vibrant. You can help me, Jacob, you can help me to live again."

He reached out, and his iron grasp clamped upon my arm. I almost accepted defeat but then from behind us, the books began to fly from the shelves and in the confusion, a strong shove in the back propelled me forward and towards the front door. I grappled with the handle, fumbling at the lock, and as I did so, I saw behind me, reflected in the windowpane, the pale face of Mr Hogarth. "Go!" he mouthed. And I ran.

And so, packing my boxes today, once more on the move, I remembered Hogarth and Eden books, and Paradise Street. Again, the same feeling of dread swept over me. I glanced again at the poetry anthology, and as I did so, a book on the very top of the box caught my eye. It was Hogarth's own book, the only one he had finished, a copy I had secured from a charity shop. It was titled *Dark Entity* and was the story of an unknown creature that stalked the centuries, surviving on the life-energy of others. I shuddered, yet I reflected that, unlike Hogarth, I did finish my books, had seen them published. I remembered Mary, though, whom I had never seen again after that night. I do not know what became of Carstairs Nile or Janet Underworth. For all I know, they might still be at Eden books, draining the energy out of more hapless victims, just enough to let them live, and in the process, crushing their hopes, dreams and ambitions. I do not know if James Hogarth will ever rest in peace.

I took one last glance at my lined and drawn face in the mirror, which I then removed from the wall and packed away. Outside, the van had arrived to take my belongings to my new destination. And so, alone, I went along the hallway and opened the front door.

The Bog-Man

The wind whipped all around, lashing the sides of the ship and tossing it about on the ocean as if it were a lost toy. Dark clouds gathered, and the horizon dipped in and out of view. Miniature whirlwinds sprang up from the sea, and then erupted in blizzards of foam. The storm outside raged on incessantly; it was as if the gods had decreed that the mortals would suffer, that their journeys would be perilous and uncomfortable and not for the faint-hearted.

Amelia turned over in the hard bed, in the cramped cabin her husband had booked for them many months before. She groaned, sweating and chilled in equal measure. Every motion of the ship, every quick vibration and every smooth slide across the waves brought with it fresh and unabated nausea. She lurched to the cabin bathroom and heaved once more over the sink. All sense of decorum deserted her now, and she was glad her husband had left the cabin. If he could see her now, thought Amelia, he would surely regret ever having set eyes on her. What a sorry sight she must be! Black, running mascara, hair plastered to her head as if it were painted onto a Kewpie doll; half-dressed, slip up around her waist; enduring endless crashing waves of disorientation and dizziness. She shivered and shook like an opium addict but her fix of normality was far away; she was adrift.

Amelia had become Mrs John Seymour ten months ago. It had been a short engagement. Marriage weighed heavily upon her; she viewed it with a grave sense of responsibility. Flippancy was not in the nature of Lady Amelia Brocklehurst, and once she had decided to make a commitment to Major John Seymour, she pursued the role with the kind of dedication and passion usually reserved for a child prodigy auditioning for a prestigious conservatoire. Seymour had courted her with reserved propriety, befitting a gentleman of his status. She could not deny that the idea of marriage had filled her with a strange kind of anticipation, a need for a fulfilment that she could not explain, much less understand, but it was confined to the abstract and stopped short of reality. Other girls in her school year had nodded and winked knowingly; they seemed to have knowledge of the male sex that had passed her by. Amelia knew she was considered beautiful, a desirable catch for any mate. She had fashionable short blonde hair like Gloria Swanson, tightly curled into a glossy bob that kissed and caressed her face like the feathers of an angel's wings. She had been a model student at her finishing school, modest, gaining a deportment ribbon in her first term; a triumph in her first season. She was the belle of her coming-out ball; a sought-after prize. Amelia knew she had a role to play and play it she must. Her future was defined for her and she would live out her role to the end of her days.

The wedding had been quite a lavish show. All stops pulled out, so to speak. Her mother was delighted with her choice of husband and had insisted on accompanying her absolutely everywhere she needed to go in preparation for the event. When she chose the dress, her mother was there. When she picked the veil, her mother insisted that the family lace was woven into it. Until they realised that it was yellowing and rather brittle. This discovery induced much fussing and flapping and necessitated a trip to the dressmaker to choose new lace but not before her mother had insisted that they at least tried a bit of Reckitt's Blue to whiten the original. It ended up becoming part of a lace handkerchief, tucked under her dress strap, to form the requisite 'something old' and 'something borrowed' in one.

When the big day arrived, Amelia felt numb. It was like observing someone else's life. Still, it marked a rite of passage into adulthood, whatever that meant. The church bells rang out, the nervous bride approached the altar with the appropriate amount of blush to her cheek, and the groom, that rather inconsequential addition to the event, turned to tell her that she looked beautiful. Yes, this was truly the first day of her independent life.

What Irony! Not long after the day's frivolities, the expectation that her life would somehow begin evaporated. Her mother had given her a 'little talk' the night before the wedding and had left her a book beside the cramped single bed in her childhood room. Having looked through it, Amelia had to admit that she hoped he would drink enough alcohol to render him very sleepy. On the wedding night, she changed into her satin gown, helped herself to the champagne left by the bedside, and waited for John to come up from the bar. The marriage had been consummated that night in sleepy, drunken haste and Amelia lay in the dark, hours after her husband had begun snoring beside her, wondering if this was all she had to look forward to.

She had anticipated a slightly more luxurious or perhaps leisurely, honeymoon. It had already been delayed by John's work by some few months and now, here they were, on a ship, combining his work with their honeymoon. Not ideal. Since they had arrived onboard, she had barely had an opportunity to speak to him alone other than in bed, and to be honest, they didn't speak much then. She was beginning to understand that she didn't really know him properly at all. John had the bags carried upstairs to the room, and left Amelia with them, explaining that he had to pop downstairs to have a chat with some of his colleagues, in the bar below, about an impending expedition.

John was an archaeologist, an explorer. He gave lectures at museums, he gave lectures at the university and quite often, he gave lectures at home. Amelia already knew better than to object to his desertion that night so she simply nodded her assent. The heavy, sinking feeling that she felt now, as she vomited into the toilet bowl onboard the ship, where she felt imprisoned, had begun on her wedding night and never left her.

Would this sickness never end? And where was her husband? Amelia crawled back into bed, remembering the promises he had made her that this would be an opportunity to see another part of the world and assuring her that he had never suffered from seasickness and it was very rare to encounter a storm on the little passage they had to make. She had waited so long for her honeymoon, and now it was yet another weary disappointment. She sipped her water and popped the little pill given to her by the ship's doctor and tried to sleep.

John suddenly burst into the room and startled her out of her sickly reverie.

"They want him, Amelia! By God, they want him!"

"How long do I have to endure this boat, John, I feel terrible!"

"It's a ship, Amelia, a ship," he said, frowning at her. "Well, it will be a while before we arrive but we are making a little stop in about eight hours' time. Give us a chance to see some sights."

"Yes, I hope so," she slurred drowsily, "it is our honeymoon after all." Then she realised exactly what he had said. "Want whom, John?"

John looked at her with an expression of incredulity. "Surely you can't mean to say that you haven't taken in a word of what I have been saying to you for the past six months?"

She stared at him blankly.

"They…the museum…want our specimen. The man from the bog? The peat bog man? The one I have been working on for so long? You know he is onboard the ship, yes?" He frowned at her in impatient disapproval again, but then a small, thin smile appeared. "A piece of history travelling with us. Oh, Amelia we are so lucky to have him! Imagine if he had got into the wrong hands? There are those who would not have appreciated him, his beauty."

"I haven't seen him yet," replied Amelia, uncertainly.

"Oh! My dear! But you must. He is so beautifully preserved. Even the contents of his stomach can tell us what his last meal was. He is thousands of years old. It is so exciting!"

Amelia thought about why she married John, as whatever remained of the contents of her own stomach shifted again. Surely, this enthusiasm must have been part of his attraction? Somehow, it ignited, just briefly, a spark in her. She considered it, then it was gone. The flame extinguished. She was sharing her honeymoon with a dead man from a bog, and he caused more animation in her husband than she had seen throughout their entire relationship.

And then it struck her that this trip was absolutely nothing to do with her and everything to do with this 'specimen.' Thousands of years buried, and now, here he was, this 'bog-man' who had delayed their honeymoon. She had married an explorer, an archaeologist, and that was the plain and simple fact of the matter.

"I *would* like to see him," she stated.

"I will take you there. If you are sure you are feeling a bit better, my dear?"

Amelia assented, and so the deal was done.

Daunting though it was, she put on a brave front. Feeling slightly nauseous still, she followed her husband into the bowels of the ship. As the door swung open, she had no idea what to expect. Would he be horrifying? Revolting? She found it problematic to assign him the pronoun, to imagine him as once-living. To her he was just a thing, an 'it'. She expected a monster.

Strangely though, her first sight was compelling, fascinating. She beheld not a monster but something peculiarly human, something almost comforting. Here was a man, who had once walked the same earth as she, who had once breathed the same air as she. He precipitated a consideration of her mortality, to question what is human, to

31

what worth does the sum of our entire deeds amount? Thinking about it made her entire world shift on its axis; she felt ridiculously dizzy and asked if she might sit.

"Oh, I'm so sorry. I'm being very thoughtless," said John, trying to convey his sympathy with a contorted little frown of what he imagined showed concern. "You must feel terrible, and he's not really a pretty sight if you aren't used to this sort of thing."

"On the contrary," replied Amelia, "I think he is rather compelling. It's just..." She couldn't articulate exactly what he made her feel, so she gave up. She simply stared at the creature.

"He seems as if he is asleep, like he could wake at any minute and get up and walk about. I know it sounds silly but are you sure you've done the right thing, digging him up? It's...well it's a bit like grave robbing, surely?" She turned to John, her face concerned.

"Now, Amelia, would you say that we shouldn't have uncovered the Egyptian tombs either? All that history, undiscovered. How on earth would we ever learn anything?" he retorted, somewhat defensively.

Amelia felt a bit ridiculous and unsure again. "I expect you're right," she acquiesced, "but you told me people died after the Pharaohs' tombs were opened like a curse was upon them, some sort of judgement. And where did all the artefacts go? Didn't some of them get stolen?"

John looked at her with something like disdain mingled with pity. "Really," he said, "you have to let go of these archaic sentimental ideas. They are not rooted in science but simply theological hocus pocus, designed to keep us living in fear. Judgement indeed."

But Amelia was uneasy and John's scornful logic could not quell the feeling. She began to scrutinise the creature, taking in every inch of him. His face was like old, brown leather, weather-beaten as if he had spent too much time in the sun. His face was so lined and creased, yet at the same time, strangely shiny. He did look as if he was sleeping, creased leather eyelids shut over almost empty sockets. His body still bore clothing, cloth sacking, crusted with ancient, dried mud, slightly whitened over time like clay. The peat bog had preserved every detail perfectly, so that the ancient man looked wizened but oddly new, and as if he belonged in this modern setting as much as he belonged to a long-past age. He did not seem as if he had been in pain when he died, his face was peaceful. Death had marked his expression with his last dream; who could imagine those final images as a human life drifts suspended between reality and oblivion, all thoughts becoming fluid as the starry edges of existence fade away?

Perhaps, she thought, he met with a violent end? Maybe he died in battle or was murdered. Could they tell? It didn't seem so but she would ask John if he had evidence of it. Death, when he comes, may be the greatest deceiver. What looked like peace could conceal torture, making this once-man relieved to draw his final breath and find peace. She looked at the rest of his body. He had lain, originally, in the foetal position, slightly curled, spine making a perfect curve into his legs and ending in small and leathery feet. John's team had taken great care when they moved him, and he was back in that childlike shape now, although she felt, again quite irrationally, that he had suffered since his resurrection. They had prodded and cut him, investigating him like an experiment. They knew his last meal, had taken the contents of his stomach and examined them. Bread, nuts and seeds of some sort; did he know, at the time, that he would never eat again? Amelia could not articulate any of the things she felt at that moment, except that she suddenly felt quite angry with John.

"He's a person," she protested. "I didn't expect to see a person. He's had a name and a life. You have taken something from him; you have taken his history and his dignity and you have decimated his peaceful resting place. I don't care whether or not you think I am being 'sentimental', I only know that I just think it's wrong. What if someone dug you up centuries later? How would you feel?"

John stared at her in disdain. "Amelia, I would not 'feel' anything of course. Don't be so silly. He is dead. He has the great honour of not dying in vain; he holds a small key to our past. We can learn so much from him."

"But the question is John," she pursued, "should we?"

She turned on her heel and entered the stairwell, beginning now the long ascent to the deck. She needed air. Her sickness had vanished quite abruptly, replaced with another sort of sick feeling. Maybe she was being irrational, but she felt it. And there was something else, a sort of dread. She didn't know why but she felt as if there would be retribution for John's bodysnatching. As she stepped out onto the swaying deck, she watched the grey skyline and the horizon appear and disappear rhythmically, all the time checking for signs of impending disaster. And she was inexplicably afraid.

Later that day, the ship pulled into a dock to make a stop. Amelia was sitting in the bar, sipping at a gin and tonic, into which someone had plopped a lemon and an olive. She supposed that it was meant to imbue it with sophistication but she hated the idea of food in her drink, although she didn't have the heart to tell the barman. She heard the low drone of the ship's engines change gear and slow and as they did so, a confusing babble of voices and busy streets began to grow loud. She slid off her barstool and headed for the window to see where they were docking. Perhaps she should go up on deck? They were probably going to have to leave the ship now, so it might be a good idea to gain a sense of place before they arrived properly. But at that moment, John burst into the bar.

"Gather up your things old girl!" he shouted, jovially. "We're going to explore a bit. The ship's stopping over for a while because I have to talk to the museum director about our precious cargo. If all goes well, we should be able to offload him here, give him a new home, eh?"

"I thought you said they wanted him?" said Amelia in surprise.

"Yes, they do," replied John, "but they have to have a look at him, and I have to talk money with them."

The streets were filled with garish colours, packed with a cacophony of endless chatter and blaring horns, producing anything but a euphonic symphony. Flags flapped in the light breeze and market traders tried tirelessly to out-do each other in an attempt to part the buyer with his cash. They knew they had rich pickings, as the typical travellers were well-heeled, desperate to impress and easily fooled by the promise of a trinket gilded with the mystic lacquer of an exotic land. Amelia, who was not a seasoned traveller, felt that every sense had been assaulted at once. This was her first 'grand tour'; she had not embarked on the fashionable endeavour before like so many of her kind. She was excited and appalled all at once. The heat had enveloped her and made it difficult to breathe. But she felt swept along by the current of sweat and exotic incense and she was literally being dragged by the hand by her enthusiastic husband as if he were an unruly puppy.

On and on through the crowds, they pushed until at last, they reached the museum in the square. It was an imposing white building flanked by outlandish Doric columns and a sweeping staircase inviting the casually uninitiated and expert alike to enter.

Amelia considered that the real power of the museum was to render its contents powerless. Even the most important deity, a statue of an ancient god or some other totem with priceless value to the people of its culture, lost the power to frighten or amaze when safely contained within its sterile walls and became simply a spectacle of art akin to that of the freak show so popular in the last century. The viewer could simply gawp and offer platitudes disguised as intellectual analysis. Amelia hoped she could find something intelligent to say.

Approaching them was a stocky and dishevelled man in crumpled linens. He had a genial countenance with few lines, although he was obviously not young. He loped over to them with a strange, awkward gait. Although he looked like an unlikely candidate, Amelia realised that he must be the museum director. He looked like he would have difficulty getting dressed in the morning but Amelia supposed that this must be the foible of the intellectual art historian, the 'mad professor type'. This nomenclature did not apply to her husband; he was more of the 'bootlegger' type. She watched John arrange his face into the appropriate congenial expression and extend his hand ready to greet this unassuming academic.

"Percival! Delightful to see you as always old fellow!" exclaimed John enthusiastically.

"Likewise, John. How have you been?"

"Very well. Very well, indeed. Look here, you haven't met my wife. Percival Hammond, this is Amelia."

Amelia extended a nervous hand but Percival clasped both of her hands like a kindly uncle.

"My dear, I am so sorry I could not come to your wedding. I hope you will forgive me. So lovely to meet you at last," he said.

Something about his manner made Amelia want to cry. It was a long time since she had felt so warmly received. She hoped that her eyes did not glisten too obviously.

Percival muttered something about tea but John insisted that they should discuss the real purpose of the visit.

"Of course," said Percival, "the others will be here shortly, so let's have some refreshments and then we can get down to it. I am so excited to see him! Is he really as well preserved as you say?"

"Percival," replied John, "he looks as if he could walk off that ship!"

The two of them then appeared to become more business-like and Amelia's concentration wandered. Suddenly, she was aware of John's voice.

"Darling, you look bored with this male talk. Why don't you have a wander around the museum?"

"Goodness, yes!" interjected Percival. "It has three floors and it is terribly interesting; I have personally contributed thousands of artefacts to the collections."

So, Amelia made a polite exit from the money-dominated conversation and started to meander around the enormous, impressive building. It seemed to her that, although the rooms were filled with artefacts and relics from times long past, they had the power to bring her to life and to connect with her. She imagined the long-dead mummy, in his decorative sarcophagus, reaching out to her across time and space; she could almost feel his breath close to her. She imagined his desperate tales of love and life, whispering to her, advising and directing her. The smell of polish and dust was not an altogether unpleasant aroma; it reminded her of her schooldays.

But slowly, a creeping melancholy began to oppress her, sweeping over her like a dark sky. She felt almost suffocated among these artefacts; stuffed birds menaced her from the high glass cases, broken pottery, limbless statues and other strange specimens loomed out at her from shadowy alcoves. Tigers hid in dark corners, poised to pounce. Now she imagined the mummies as sentient vampires, thinking about their resurrection. Her head began to pound. She listened and followed the echoing guffaws of John and Percival until she was with them again.

"Back so soon, my dear?" smiled John, condescendingly. "It's a rather big museum you know."

"I...yes, I know, however, I am still feeling a little unwell, and I think I may have to return to the ship," she replied.

John's brow creased and he turned to his companion. "She is not a seasoned seafarer, Percival." He turned back to Amelia, and replied, "Well, if you must, of course. I'm sorry to hear that." He seemed to her to be irritated. "Fetch the guide, Percy," he commanded. "Percival's guide will see you safely back to the ship, my dear, where you must lie down and recover."

The guide soon appeared, dishevelled but looking cooler than the British party. Amelia gave him a watery smile and followed where he beckoned.

Again, they were in the hot, oppressive crowds, travelling through the dusty streets, which were now slightly shadowed as the sun continued its heavenly arc. There was no respite from the heat, from the headache and feeling of unease that Amelia could not shake off. She was thankful when the white giant of the ship came into view again, despite its ability to sicken her to the stomach when in motion, and she longed to return to her cabin and shut the door. She knew she could not close the door on her thoughts but perhaps she would slip back into sleep and be relieved by some lighter dreams. She thanked the guide and headed back to rest.

Sometime later, Amelia awoke with a start. It was now dark, and she had slept fitfully. There were no clear, defined dreams that she remembered, only hazy fragments at the corners of her memory which quickly dissolved on waking, disappearing like dust on the breeze. Thirsty and aching, she rose from the bed and padded into the bathroom to fetch a glass of water. As she did so, it suddenly struck her that John (And indeed Percival) had not yet returned. This was odd because she knew that they were coming back to view the 'Bog man' as she had come to think of him.

A strange knot began to form in her stomach.

She peered out of the cabin door into the moonlight, which was now shrouded in a faint mist, giving the moon a watery appearance. Cautiously, she reached back, slipped on a light coat and stepped out onto the deck. The ship appeared to be in darkness and felt deserted. Now the knot inside her began to tighten. She slowly began to make her way along the deck. The stillness was chilling and although very faint sounds were just audible in the distance, the hubbub of the marketplace had died down and the air was bird-less. As Amelia tiptoed further, she suddenly slipped.

Looking down, she saw, in the moonlight, a thick, sticky pool, steaming beneath her feet. It looked like offal and she realised that the slippery mass was blood and entrails. She heard peculiar noises coming from her own throat as she backed up, scraping and scraping at her slipper to try to get it off and get away from the revolting mess. Gagging and retching in disgust, she blindly tried to run anywhere on the deck and began to shout to anyone who might hear her. Where were the crew?

The black sea crashed around her and suddenly, a torrential wave washed over the side of the boat and showered Amelia. In the icy shock, she bolted for the stairwell and ran down and down until she was once again outside the door where the long-dead man dwelt.

For an inexplicable reason, Amelia felt drawn by some instinct to go through that door once more. Very cautiously, she pushed it open to enter the temporary tomb. When she did so, she was unprepared for the sight that greeted her: the case was empty, and the man was gone.

Amelia stifled a scream and without thinking, fled from the room and back up to the deck in a blind panic. When she reached the outside, where by now rain had begun to fall heavily, she finally screamed and screamed, without stopping.

"Amelia, Amelia! Whatever is the matter?" It was John, returning with Percival.

"Oh, John! Oh!" She ran into his arms. "The man from the bog, he's gone, he's gone, he's alive I know it, I found blood, the crew have gone...I...I..."

She could say no more, trying to point to where she had slipped. But the deck was awash with seawater and rain and no trace of what she had seen remained.

Back in the lounge area, with the lights burning once more, Amelia sat, with a brandy, relating what had happened to Percival and John. John sat impassively, his fingers pressed together, eyes half-closed and never interrupting. When she had finished, he spoke.

"Amelia, I gave the crew shore leave. I am so sorry; I did not consider your feminine fragility and sensitive nature. I should never have let you return to the ship to rest alone. I could see you were overwhelmed and exhausted." He turned to Percival. "It was so remiss of me. It is well known, is it not, that women have such lurid imaginations, always prone to the fanciful. I never considered it in my own wife but I should have done."

"Well, it is true that the fairer sex can be more sensitive," said Percival, "whereas we might be more inclined to pursue a rational explanation. But I am not sure this entirely applies to your wife here. I confess, I hardly know her but she seems to be a sensible and intelligent woman." He smiled kindly at Amelia. "She is probably very overtired and recovering from that awful seasickness, aren't you, my dear?" Percival patted her hand. Then he addressed John, with a serious expression. "However," he said, "don't you think we should go downstairs and just check that our prize has not, indeed, gone?"

"I'm coming with you," said Amelia, "I'm not staying here alone."

The three of them made their way down to the bottom of the ship once more. When they entered the room, Amelia gasped.

"There. Everything is in order. I suppose you can have a good look at him now, Percy."

"Indeed, he is a fine specimen. Looks alive. So well-preserved," replied a delighted Percival.

"But…" faltered Amelia, "he wasn't there."

John took her gently by the hand and suggested that she might return to the cabin for rest. "It's nothing more than an over-active mind, brought on by the trial of your travel and tiredness, dearest," he reassured her, "let's all stay on the ship tonight, as I planned, Percy, and we can take a proper look at him in the morning."

As he led them all back up, Amelia glanced back at the man from the bog, still sleeping in his case. She thought she saw something different in him, an angle of his head, perhaps? A trace of water on his cheek? Were his lids half-open, giving the impression that he was watching them all? She tried to dismiss these intrusive thoughts and followed the men, where, outside her cabin, she bid them goodnight and then firmly locked her door behind her, knowing that John would not come to bed for quite some time.

As the night wore on, the strange stillness of earlier had gone; the rain intensified, smashing insistently on the tiny portholes. A faint sound of thunder rumbled ominously in the distance and sudden flashes of lightning streaked the sky. Amelia slept fitfully, dreaming of the bog man's brown, leathery face. In her dreams, she saw him leaning over her;

felt his hot, foul breath on her face as if it were real. A loud knocking on her cabin door woke her with a start.

"Amelia, let me in!" cried John. "Amelia, I can't find Percy! The ship's rocking all over the place! Amelia! Wake up!"

Her heart knocking at her ribs, Amelia flung open the cabin door. Although by now, it must be approaching the early hours of dawn, darkness still swelled around them solidly. On John's face, illuminated by the weak moonlight, she saw only blind panic.

"Thank God, you are all right!" he shouted through the sound of the storm. "Amelia, Percy left the lounge where we were drinking and he did not return! I don't know what to do! What if he's been washed over the side?"

A feeling of dread consumed Amelia. She slipped on her robe and slippers once more and trailing damp silk behind her, she dragged John by both hands out onto the deck again.

"We have to find him! He's in danger, there's no time to lose!" she cried.

She had never seen her rational, emotionless husband in such a terrified state. He seemed not to comprehend her at first but then followed her, calling out for Percy all the time.

They ran, slipping and sliding around the sodden deck. Up more stairs, down staircases, calling and searching until, at last, they were inevitably back outside the room of the dead man again.

This time, Amelia did not hesitate to fling the door wide open and there, the sight that greeted them both stopped their breath in horror: the case was empty! All that remained was the indent of the body; the muslin sheets which had surrounded him were damp and stained with traces of blood.

Amelia did not freeze, did not really think. She grasped John by both hands and took him back up to the deck.

"We're leaving this ship! I think he's got all of the crew, they are not coming back, John. And I think he's got Percy. If we don't leave now, I think we will be next!"

"What? You've gone mad! The crew are on leave. Percy must have slipped overboard. We have to find him!" John yelled at her.

"I don't want to die!" she screamed. "Come with me! I'm leaving now!" Amelia pleaded but John would not budge. He would not believe it. So, with one last pleading glance, she slipped her hand away from his. As she did so, her wedding ring crashed to the deck and rolled over the side, into the swirling blackness below.

Amelia began to run for the gangplank. A thousand thoughts spun around in her head. None of it made sense but she knew she was running for her life. As she reached the exit though, she heard a terrifying masculine cry. It was human but sounded like an inhuman roar. Amelia turned back to see two shadows on the deck above, wrestling with one another by the rail.

She did not really stop to think. In no time, she had made her way back up to John and when she reached him, her blood ran cold. He was locked in combat with a leathery, wizened creature who appeared to be clawing, biting and ripping at his body causing him to yell in pain and terror as he tried to fight back. Amelia reached the first thing to hand, a lantern hanging outside the quarter-deck. She held it aloft, illuminating the scene. The creature was arrested in his attack and turned to face her. In that moment, Amelia saw something in his face. She saw not a creature, not a monster but a man once more; a man, whose face was hungry, anguished and pained. As he looked upon her, his expression seemed to soften and without speaking, he spoke to her across the centuries.

Amelia knew what she had to do. As the bog-man stood distracted, he loosened his grip and she seized John away to safety behind her with strength she did not know she possessed. John could only gawp, open-mouthed, as she took hold of this terrible, beautiful creature.

"I know you should not be here. I release you," she told it, yelling through the wind. "He was wrong, I hear you. I release you." And with a gentle push, she sent the man from the past down into the foaming waves.

"Amelia! Our prize!" yelled John. "What have you done?"

"Even now?" cried Amelia through the blackness. "Can't you see you should never have taken him, John?"

She stared at John for a few more seconds. She felt momentarily sorry for him. His face had lost its usual self-assured expression. All traces of arrogance and self-righteousness were gone and in their place was a pained look of defeat and desperation. Her time with him flickered through her mind like a projected film, and for her future, she saw only neutral tones, as dead as the man she had just released into the sea should have remained. Slowly, she raised herself up onto the railings, peering down into the dark waters and for a second, she paused, thinking she heard the creature calling out to her. Then abruptly she let go and launched herself into the black water below and was gone.

John stood alone on the deck in disbelief and for hours afterwards, even when help arrived, he stood watching the grey clouds amassing like an army in the coming dawn.

Reflection

Sitting in front of the mirror has been my life's preoccupation. Here, today, staring at my reflection again, I barely recognise myself. As ever, I am completely absorbed, drawn in to inspect every detail. My sense of self is disappearing as the face reflected back seems unfamiliar as if there are two of us, the one here outside the mirror and the one on the other side of the glass, looking out.

If I narrow my eyes, I can almost imagine that my surroundings darken and recede into the background; the face on the other side appearing to move independently of my own. The stranger raises an eyebrow or blinks, imperceptibly. I cannot believe the withered and haggard reflection that stares back. I am certain that there is a new line, a new hollowing of the flesh every day. Dark circles frame sunken eyes; cheekbones sit sharply, like wishbones, on the pinched, cadaverous face; the complexion is sallow, like wax in danger of melting and descending in offensive drips to the floor.

It was not always like this.

As a flaxen-haired child in the nursery, my nanny told me every day that I was the most beautiful boy she had ever seen. I was an angel sent from heaven, and surely, she always repeated, to my parents' distress, I must have been sent only on loan as I was far too beautiful to live. Unlike my poor parents, I did not spend anxious months awaiting my imminent demise, where I would be returned to the heavenly realm from whence I came. No, I was too young for such conceits. But I can imagine my mother harbouring doubts, however irrational, precipitated by the nanny's careless flattery, and I suppose she must have eventually allowed herself to breathe a sigh of relief when it was evident that I was to continue to survive beyond infancy.

The words, however, had obviously stayed with me in some subconscious form. Although true self-consciousness lay dormant while I was in the nursery with no one to compare myself to, this state of innocence reached an end when I was sent away to school and my world grew larger.

I measured my beauty against others and I noticed that physical beauty was powerful. Others gravitated towards me as if I emitted a magnetic force, drawing them in. Most wanted to join my circle, hoping that some of my sheen would rub off on their lacklustre selves and lend them a polished gloss of their own. I did not have friends; I had admirers. But if they were sycophants, I chose to ignore it. Like the proverbial cat, I walked alone and I was the king of all I surveyed.

My hair grew paler, my eyes more piercing. While others suffered blemishes, not a single spot marred my smoothness. I examined my face on a daily basis, each time spending perhaps a little longer gazing at my reflection than the last. I saw only positive changes, as I grew more defined from a boy to a youth and to a man.

My passage from school to university followed as I excelled in academia. My followers from school dispersed but new ones appeared in their wake in a small, elite circle. It was soon no surprise that I was sought after by young women but I did not encourage their company, content to bask in my own glory, each day the mirror reflecting back my only desire. Until one chance encounter.

My university had staged a publicity event, just after graduation, to showcase the academic elite. I was sauntering aimlessly across the cobbled courtyard in early July, when I was approached by a smart young woman, brandishing a cumbersome camera. She told me she worked for *The Echo* newspaper and asked if she might take my photograph and interview me.

Naturally, I obliged. I was intrigued by this beauty and she had been flattering. But she was also earnest and unusual, her flattery was sincere and she was not, as was usually the case, overawed by my looks but interested in my work. It was an odd sensation; I had briefly walked with the mortals. At the same time, it presented a challenge, I felt deflated by it. This woman's reaction to me had singled her out as unique. I was determined to find out more and after the story was printed, I contacted her.

It was at the end of August, one languid afternoon, when we lay on my bed by an open-sash window in my attic room, filled with wine, high above the sweating city. The heat was overpowering but there was an air of sadness. I was soon to leave my rooms and the cosseted university life. The sweltering sky threatened to split into a thunderstorm. We sucked on our cigarettes and sipped wine as she traced my profile with her finger, suggesting that I had been chiselled by the gods. I laughed at this profundity and told her that I marvelled at the way she rarely spoke like this; surprised she placed intellect above my looks unlike everyone I had ever known. Then she uttered words that chilled me: she told me that my remarkable looks had drawn her to me but that looks could not last. However, she would always love me, no matter what.

At that moment, it was as if a storm had struck. Something in my world shifted and the season seemed colder. I no longer wanted her company.

Over the ensuing years, I gave her little thought. I believed I remained unchanged but she would now have lost the bloom of youth. As I studied myself in my mirror now, I had no room for distractions. I was adored at work and I was a glittering social success. Life was a long series of champagne cocktails and elaborate, twinkling parties. I never lacked company and I was reassured that one thing remained constant and alluring: my reflection.

It was by chance, on one of my outings, standing by the bar of a busy art-deco establishment, that I caught a glimpse of a familiar silhouette behind me, reflected in the mirror. I turned and there she was; only this woman was not the girl I had cast aside previously. This woman was wasted and shrunken, weighed down by disappointment. She was striving to present a façade of enjoyment but she wore misery like a shroud. She gasped in astonishment at my turning, I had not changed, she told me, a little older maybe but otherwise…unscathed. Her eyes met mine, forlornly. She made excuses and hurried away before I could speak.

The encounter had disturbed me and I felt strangely bereft. That night I went back to my large, empty house. As I studied myself in the mirror this time, I conceded I was a little older but yes, mostly unchanged. However, my reflection gave me less joy than usual. For I could not befriend it, could not dine with it or laugh with it in its two-dimensional world. The seeds of discontentment had been sown. Did others see me as I saw myself? It troubled me that she had seen me ageing and I realised then that I surely must change, if not now, then inevitably as time advanced. No human is immortal and I was deluded if I believed that time would not make its mark on me.

The years passed and I began to spend longer and longer in front of my mirror until eventually, I started to notice something strange; the reflection appeared to move independently. It was barely detectible at first and I thought I must be imagining it, but as surely as night followed day, it soon became a regular occurrence. As I moved my right arm, the figure in the mirror followed. But not my matching reflection. The actual right arm of the mirrored self moved as if I had inverted and sat on the other side of the glass looking out. Other oddities followed: the blink of the wrong eye; the wrong eyebrow raised.

And each day too, I watched my reflection changing, growing older and hollower. My work no longer satisfied me and my social scene fell away. I spent increasing hours staring, examining, longing and wishing that I could connect with the forlorn figure trapped behind the glass.

Alone today in front of the mirror once more, I know that too many years have been spent pining for my lost self, losing myself in the deep pool of bevelled glass, its edges decorated with tiny white flowers. I know now that we, myself and I, can never meet. I was gifted with beauty but I have squandered my existence in search of an elusive dream and now I must confront the truth: I am old and I am alone. In anger, I take my mirror and throw it to the floor, watching myself splinter into a hundred fragments.

Instantly, I regret my action. I have lost my only friend. Yet surely that haggard, woe-begone friend was really my nemesis, who might destroy me? I run in despair to the next room, where I know I will see myself again. But in this mirror, the sight reflected back is not the one that I shattered only minutes ago. Instead, I see my youthful self, beautiful as in my prime. I put my hand to the cold glass and he does the same. My copy is no longer my true likeness but my younger self restored. Then, I am seized with a pang of fear and envy. If only I could once again be the beauty in the mirror and he be forced to live in aged misery and loneliness. I trace my fingers lovingly around his face until our fingers meet again. Strangely, the surface of the glass begins to yield like a mercurial liquid. I feel myself slowly pulled forward with gentle insistence and then my perspective changes.

In panic, I reach forward but I am stopped by the glass. I push and push, but the surface is solid again. I pound on it with my knuckles. I can see my room: the chest of drawers; the heavy, ancient wardrobe; the stippled glass above the doorframe. I place my hands flat on the surface and scream silently as I watch the young and beautiful creature on the other side straighten his tie, give me a wink, and walk away, leaving the room and closing the door behind him.

The Locked Door

The Summer was over. Anyone with only a casual glance might be forgiven for thinking it was still at its peak, as the sun had already begun his steady climb to the highest point in the sky, the rays still strong enough to radiate heat as his warm light danced over the cracked and dusty terracotta tiles on the terrace. But the days were growing shorter, the nights cooler, and there was an oppressive heaviness that hung in the air. It was the moment when the season had become like a guest who had outstayed her welcome but was reluctant to leave; the moment of over-ripeness, before the air lightened again and a fresh breeze signalled the onset of autumn's orange vibrancy.

Eleanor Pembroke was at her window in the early part of that morning, before it grew hot, looking out at the end of summer before it took flight. She could hear insects buzzing beneath the ledge; in the distance, the clock in the square chimed a quarter to nine. Alistair Pembroke was not up yet; still snoring lightly, with the covers turned back, and a fan cooling him as he slept. This was a snapshot of stillness, before he came crashing out into the day with the energy of a rampaging bull, and nowhere to direct his charge. She knew their son, Alex, was playing out in the field already, with his older brother, Jonathan. The boys loved the freedom of roaming over the vast land, which lay in its raw, unkempt state offering the promise of adventure. Eleanor closed her eyes and listened to the buzzing insects, and the wind rustling through the dry grass. She had a headache and surmised that a storm was brewing.

She could hear Elise, the cleaner, enter downstairs and begin pottering around in the kitchen. She pulled on a robe and hurried down to greet her.

"Madame! Good morning!" said Elise, enthusiastically, in her lilting French accent. "How are we today?"

It was a question that Eleanor found difficult to answer. She responded with a brief nod and mumbled "fine," and then she wandered over to the large glass doors which led out on to the veranda and gazed out, distractedly.

There was something odd about the rose bushes. Eleanor could not put her finger on it, but they seemed to have bloomed out of season, and were brighter and more colourful than they should be. Perhaps she had some sort of power over them, to make them bloom more beautifully at her will? She smiled to herself, but found the idea that she might command the flowers to bloom slightly disconcerting and dismissed it from her mind as ridiculous.

She was aware of a fly buzzing around in the kitchen. The noise might have been small and insignificant, but to Eleanor, it sounded like a chainsaw next to her ear, coming closer, and retreating; closer, and retreating again. She put her hands up to her head, covering each ear to block out the incessant noise, but it did not stop.

"What is the matter Madame?" cried Elise, looking concerned.

"Oh, the noise! C'est terrible!" Eleanor moaned.

"Let me open the windows a little more and let some fresh air in," suggested Elise gently.

"No! No! No!" Eleanor felt inexplicably terrified. The buzzing had intensified, and the walls now seemed to wobble and move inwards. "More insects will come in!"

Elise took up a broom, and with one deft move, she silenced the fly forever. Then she threw open the huge glass doors which led out onto the veranda. Eleanor could hear the distant voices of her children playing in the fields and all seemed to be calm again. She felt certain they would soon be inside, hugging her warmly. A stillness descended within her briefly.

"Why doesn't madame go back to bed for a while?" suggested Elise.

Eleanor could hear Alistair stirring now, the bed creaking as he swung out of it. Feeling an odd and overwhelming desire to hide, she agreed gratefully, and began to make her way back to the room where she had been sleeping alone for the past few months.

Her room was dark and airless; even with the window thrust wide it felt stuffy. Alistair had suggested that she stayed here to recover from her recent illness. Her memory of that illness was distorted; Alistair had told her that was because she had been so very ill, and that the medication she had been given had dulled her senses, but it was necessary to aid her complete rest and recovery. She had spent a lot of her life being told what was best for her, and her mind wandered back to her childhood.

When Eleanor was seven, she enjoyed playing alone. But there was never really anyone around to play with, as her parents had moved around so much. This house, in the tiny French village of Santenay, in the Burgundy region, had belonged to her parents, and she had inherited it. She had spent a great deal of her childhood here. There was a beautiful view of the Montagne Des Trois Croix – the Mountain of the three crosses – which could provide a panoramic view of the Loire valley when scaled on a clear day, or create drama when thunder and lightning rolled around the hills, lighting up the sky like pink fire, in stormy weather.

She had played, much as her sons played now, in the wild fields, and beside the canal, which led into the river Soane. It was idyllic. She was never lonely, as she had many imaginary friends who would keep her company. Each had a distinctive voice and personality. She invented all the voices and entertained herself all day long, amusing visitors when they came to stay.

But for some reason, her father found this excruciatingly embarrassing, and if they had guests, whether on the terrace for glasses of wine from the local vineyard, or more formal dinners inside the house, she was always instructed by her father to keep away, out of sight.

Eleanor's mother was often unwell, and regularly to be found lying down, so she did not argue much about Eleanor's banishment. It was on a warm, sunny day when her mother was taken to hospital after she had woken up in the night and had a very bad fall. Eleanor had heard the commotion, and a great deal of whispering. People came and went, and her uncle even turned up from England. She did not even get to kiss her mother before she left, although she did not really remember her mother being the kissing type. After that they returned to England and later she was told her mother was too ill to return to the family home. Eleanor visited her mother in hospital in England twice. The first time her mother appeared not to recognise her, and Eleanor certainly did not recognise her mother. The colourful woman with the red hair, had been replaced by a wasted, greying waxwork on a bed. The second time Eleanor saw her, she was hooked up to a machine, looking like a zombie, and Eleanor was frightened of her. After that she never saw her again, and her father and uncle told her that her mother had gone to heaven, and that it was for the best. After that, the two of them had decided it was 'best for her' if she went away to school. Eleanor's imaginary friends came with her, and she often talked to them in her dormitory at night; she learned to speak to them in her head, and sometimes they would get into mischief and blame Eleanor for it. Sometimes, she pretended she was one of them so she could get away with things.

Back in her room this morning, her bones ached. Her head pounded. And the skin of her wrists and arms was so sore that the sleeves of her robe hurt them. Why couldn't she remember her sickness? What medication could obliterate time and memory altogether? She sat down on the bed and stared at the window. The curtains billowed slightly in a sharp gust of much welcomed wind. But then they were still once more. Why was there no air? It felt impossible to breathe. She lay back on the bed and propped herself up on her three pillows, feeling she could get her breath better slightly raised. She tried to focus on something, as she was becoming overwhelmed with a heavy sleepiness and faint nausea. She concentrated on the corner of the room where a crack ran from the damp-stained wall, papered with blue and green peacocks, up into the white-washed stone ceiling. Even as she looked, the crack appeared to extend and widen, and she had the feeling of being drawn upwards, likely to disappear into its cavernous tear. She averted her eyes quickly, but on returning her gaze, she noticed that something had changed. Was that peacock spreading his tail into a fan before? She blinked. There it was – his tail feathers spread into lots of tiny eyes, all looking back at her. It had changed! She knew that was impossible. Yet the tiny eyes bored into hers, watching her from the wall. They seemed to be trying to communicate with her, and she began to feel lost in the sound of several voices all speaking to her at once. Two voices rose above the rest: "Mummy, come and play!"

Somewhere in the distance, she could still hear her children playing; their laughter seemed ceaseless. She wanted to go them. She tried to cry out, but her voice seemed suddenly stifled, and she felt unable to move. With a clumsy thrust of an arm which did not feel like her own, she knocked a glass of water to the floor, and it shattered with an explosive crash. Alistair and Elise quickly appeared at her side, comforting her, giving her water and stroking her hair. She felt a sharp scratch in the back of her hand, then blackness.

She awoke sometime later. It was not yet night, and she felt a little better, so she decided to venture out again, perhaps talk to her sons, who could not possibly still be out playing, as the afternoon had clouded over and the weather was taking a turn for the worse. Her room seemed duller than ever, and she eyed the wallpaper suspiciously, but it seemed ordinary enough. As she journeyed down the narrow hallway, shadows danced and flickered across the floor and walls, light and cloud competing for dominance. There was no sign of thunder yet, but it was coming, and the rain would follow.

Before she reached the kitchen, Eleanor paused outside a door. She thought she could hear whispering coming from behind it; urgent, hushed whispers. She heard a man's voice say, "It's getting worse. I don't know what I can do anymore." Was it her husband? Who was there with him? She tried the handle. It was locked. The whispering stopped. She decided she would ask Elise if she had the key.

Elise was no longer in the kitchen; indeed, the house seemed deserted. Eleanor noticed something: the kitchen clock had stopped. Had it stopped that morning? No. It was frozen at 12.45. It was past midday, of that she was certain, but it was not after midnight. She had slept for the entire morning, and now she was awake again, and seemed to be alone. The tap dripped intermittently, echoing in the vast stone room. And then she heard it. Between each echoing drip came a tick, tick, tick. The clock had stopped, but time still ticked from it with urgent insistence. And outside, she could still hear the voices of her boys, and the swish of the grass as the breeze rippled across its blades.

Footsteps on the flagstones startled her and she turned sharply.

"Oh, Elise, It's only you. Shouldn't the boys be inside now? It's brewing up a storm. And where is Alistair?"

"Don't worry yourself, Madame Eleanor, you just have a nice rest."

Eleanor noticed that the ticking was growing faster, and the room appeared to grow darker.

"Elise," she ventured, "I noticed that the room across the hallway is locked. Have you any idea where the key is? I thought I heard sounds coming from inside it."

"Don't trouble about it, Madame, I will see to it for you."

"But Elise, I'd like to go in there. Is my husband in there? I thought I heard him talking."

"Madame is getting upset. Why don't you have a lie down?"

"I don't WANT to lie down!" shouted Eleanor. "I want to see my children! I want to know why people are whispering in that room! I want to know why I can't remember anything properly! Unlock that room NOW!" She was beginning to feel hysterical, and she was dimly aware of Elise calling to Alistair in an urgent tone, "Monsieur! Come quickly! Madame is ill again!"

Eleanor was aware that she was shouting and calling to her children, but she felt separate from her own body. She looked at this hysterical woman as if from above, observing her dispassionately, as if she were a spider or a passing fly, without language, but with something beyond comprehension, omniscient and instant.

She felt herself flee from the kitchen and run to the locked door, where she watched herself kicking and kicking at it until it finally yielded.

What she saw was a woman in a bed, in a dark and stifling room. The woman reached out towards her without words. Eleanor could not grasp any root of reality.

"What are you doing here?" she gasped. "What is this?"

The woman's face was pale, with haggard, grey cheeks, wild knotted hair, and crazed eyes which pierced Eleanor with their horrifying and poignant emptiness. The voice that rasped out of her black slit of a mouth sounded inhuman.

"He's keeping me here against my will."

Eleanor suddenly noticed Alistair in the corner of the room, standing in shocked silence.

59

"Where are my children?" she screamed. "Who is this woman?"

She flew at Alistair, but she suddenly felt herself restrained, arms pinned down.

"Your children are dead!" cried the woman on the bed, and began to scream with one long high-pitched note; an animalistic cry of pain.

Eleanor struggled wildly, all the time screaming and clawing at air, and crying "Where are my boys? Someone has killed my children! What's going on?"

But then, she realised that there was only one woman in the room; one woman in the bed. It was dark and airless. The room had blue and green peacocks populating the walls, and to Eleanor they danced and pecked and spread their tail feathers in fans dotted with dark eyes. She was the woman in the bed, her wrists bandaged from self-inflicted slashes that leaked fresh blood, and in a dreadful moment of clarity, she seemed to see an image in her mind of two white coffins lowered into the ground, and a woman kneeling in a black coat, crying out for her lost family.

"Are they dead? Are they dead? Are they gone?" she repeated again and again, rocking back and forth.

"It's all right, hush now," whispered her husband, stroking her hair. "It's nobody's fault; there are no children. There never were, they don't exist, Eleanor. You never had children. You can't have children. You're not well." He sat beside the bed, holding her and weeping, as the doctor, and a nurse looked on sadly, knowing the time had come for Eleanor to leave.

The Sound of the Bell

It was nearly 2 am. Barker had arranged to meet Hill in this god-forsaken place upon the hour. He shuddered but it was not due to the inclement weather, although the night was indeed a fearful one; thunder rumbled in the distance, intermittent flashes of lightning illuminating the sky in bursts and Barker was soaked to the skin. No, it was this place that struck a chill into his bones, which travelled up his spine like icy fingertips tripping lightly over it.

With the next flash, just for those split seconds, light danced across the stones, silhouetting them against the brilliant sky like black monoliths that loomed large and ominous. Barker jumped as the tower clock chimed to mark the hour. He cursed himself for his irrational nervousness.

"That bloody Mr Dickens!" he swore out loud. "He's got everyone running scared of their own shadow!"

He felt about in his breast pocket for the bottle that Gull, the Queen's physician no less, had given him in exchange for one of his, shall we say, 'services'. There it was: tincture of laudanum. He lit a match. It promptly blew out. Again, he lit one but this time he cupped his hands around it and crouched beside one of the larger headstones for shelter. The match threw enough light for him to see what he was doing and he

61

pulled out the stopper, carefully squeezing a few drops onto his tongue to calm his fears. The match was quickly out, so he returned the bottle to his pocket and remained behind the stone, trying to keep sheltered from the constant driving rain and fierce wind.

After a while, he felt agitated again. He heard the clock chime a quarter past the hour. Where was Hill? Soon it would begin to grow light, for heaven's sake. An owl hooted and at the eerie sound, he turned and suddenly from nowhere, a skittering, squeaking pair of bats whipped past his ear, making him cry out in terror.

Now Barker was angry. The graveyard fell quiet once more. The driving rain had eased and the lightning seemed to have ceased. He exhaled slowly but he still started at every sound: a rustle of trees in the breeze; the snap of a twig; the rattle of the huge iron gate on its hinges.

His mind worked feverishly, conjuring black forms in the darkness, rising from their graves and gliding towards him with the intent to do harm. He fancied then that he heard the gate creak and the soft sound of footsteps somewhere in the darkness. He cowered, pulling his muffler and greatcoat closer, trying to make himself invisible to any spirit that might walk abroad. But he was well aware that it was not the dead he should fear the most. He knew that he should not be here, that what he was about to do was wrong. He should be afraid for his mortal soul but he was not so theologically inclined; if he was caught, he would surely swing for the act and this was his most pressing concern as the sky was beginning to lighten.

But the footsteps were not in his imagination. At last, Hill appeared, first as a grey shadow, then more distinct, and soon he was right beside Barker.

"What the hell you doing crouched down there? You look as white as a sheet. Seen a ghost, have yer?" Smirked Hill.

"I just don't like this creeping around cemeteries. And you're late! It'll get light in a minute and we'll be done for." Barker returned. "Anyways, it's a hell of a night; picked the worst night in about six months to come out in. I'm bloody well soaked."

"Tell you what? Go home then! You won't be getting the cash, though, if you do."

Barker knew Hill was bluffing. He wouldn't be able to do all the work himself and he had told him as much.

"Look," said Hill, "there's no use arguing when we ain't got much time. We both want the money. I know you've only been out on this a couple of times but you can't tell me you didn't find the money handy. We can't let a little thing like the weather stop us. Come on, what do you say we get to work? You know I came good with the money, I ain't gonna rip you off, am I? And while there's a market for 'em with them students and the like, we can provide the service."

Barker hesitated still. It was a foul night and boded very ill.

"Look, come on mate, we've been paid half of it," cajoled Hill, "have to give it back if we don't come up with the goods now, won't we? And I've already spent it. Look, I'm sorry I kept yer waitin'. I had a little deal to do down near the Lyric for some actor type, Richard someone, I forget who but it doesn't matter, I'm here now and Dr posh-knobs wants his goods."

Barker grimaced, remembering 'Dr Posh-knobs' from earlier on in the day. They had been lurking behind the dustbins around the back of St Barts. A very well-dressed fellow came sidling up, looking all around him, all 'cloak and dagger', thought Barker. The well-dressed man might have carried a cane and might have been wearing a top hat but he looked as furtive as any thief in Whitechapel. He stopped near to where Barker and Hill were loitering.

"Excuse me, gentleman," he said, "but do either of you have the time? Foul day, isn't it? I'm as cold as a corpse." He laughed a weak, affected laugh.

"We ain't got a watch but the sun's going down soon," replied Hill with a knowing wink. This greeting was the agreed code.

"All right gentlemen, it's a pleasure to be acquainted with you," replied the well-dressed fellow. "We need just two for tonight, fresh and in good condition. I am reliably informed that you are fellows we can trust, therefore I am entrusting you both with half of the payment now, and the rest upon delivery in the early hours. You know where to go. Booth and I will let you in."

Barker had done this before with Hill and it had turned out well. It wasn't the greatest job, a bit disgusting really but good money. Could be funny at times. How he had laughed, with relief really, the first time he'd been out. The bloody body, none too fresh, had kind of exploded on them when they put it in the barrel.

"That was 'orrible but dead funny," Hill had said, then realising the grim pun, laughed. Barker had grimaced and told him not to give up his day job to join the music hall anytime soon, which had them rolling about in the mud with the idea of a 'day job', their day job being at night.

Barker didn't know why, perhaps it was the storm that had disturbed him so much but this time it had a bad feeling about it. Then when Hill was late, he'd wondered if he'd already been caught. Even worse, there were others in the trade who were beginning to get a bit of a name for themselves. There were two of them whose names were very well associated with digging up corpses, and one of those two might have got hold of Hill. Barker dreaded to think of what they might have done to him. No scruples at all that pair, he shuddered.

But the previous afternoon had seen a hanging and a couple of fresh burials. Nobody in particular, no one who mattered. So, here were Hill and Barker, ready to free them from their eternal resting place, to be put to good use. And let's face it, without the likes of them, there wouldn't be all sorts of things in existence to help sick people. He and Hill were only doing a job, like anyone else. Some folks would say it was against God, an evil act, disturbing the dead. But from what Barker had seen in his life so far, there was no such thing as God. Where was God when his old man was coughing his lungs up, wasting away with sickness? And then they took away the costermonger's living, made it illegal long enough for most of Hill's family to starve. Where was this God then eh?

No, Barker had no moral issues with his employment. But this fiendish night felt ominous and the feeling was inexplicable.

He got back to the task. After selecting the fresh mound, they had set to work. The spades went down, the dirt piled up, and the rain ran down their necks. Eventually, they hit the cheap wood.

"Give me the crowbar, Barker!" commanded Hill.

Barker obliged and they both prised the lid off the coffin. They were blasted by the foul stink of the dead, even this new one had already started to turn. The face bore a purplish hue and was shiny like marble. He was already slightly bloated, swollen and ripe-looking. Around the neck, which lay at an odd angle, there were the tell-tale marks of the rope.

"This is the hung bloke," commented Hill, needlessly. And they began to drag him up and load him into the bag and then the barrel, ready to roll him down the road to the hospital without anyone suspecting a thing.

When they had loaded him up, Hill said they had better get on with the second one and take off as quickly as they could. But Barker had stopped, standing seemingly transfixed by something.

"Did you hear that?" he whispered. "I can hear a bell or something. Do you think someone's coming?"

"Dunno. I can't hear it," replied Hill, "but we'd better get a move on."

"Look, we'd better go," said a worried Barker, "let's just leave it and give 'em what we've got."

"No chance! I want my money!" said Hill.

They were just about to move to the next grave, when they both heard it: a distinct tinkling bell, coming from the direction in which they were heading.

Hill dropped his spade in fright. "A bloody bell!" he said. "What the hell is going on?"

"It's coming from our grave!" said Barker. "It's the angels! God forgive me!"

"There are no angels," said Hill, albeit shakily, "that's what you've always said. It ain't nothing. Let's get on with it and get out of here."

The two men took up their spades and began to dig. Both could hear the bell quite distinctly now and both carried out their task in great haste, trying to ignore the ringing, which seemed to be coming from the tombstone itself.

Finally, they hit the coffin. They looked at one another.

"Oh, give it here!" said Hill impatiently. But before he could lever the lid off completely, there began a scratching and knocking sound. And then came a muffled voice from within.

Barker began to scramble to his feet, with incoherent mutterings. He backed away in trepidation. Hill too began to back off.

Suddenly, the lid burst off and the body within sat bolt upright and reached towards the two men, gasping great gulps of air.

Hill and Barker did not wait to see what happened next. They dropped their tools, abandoned their other prize and took off across the cemetery as fast as whippets, screaming as they went, not caring whom they should wake with the noise.

If they had stayed, they would have seen a confused, panic-stricken man frantically claw his way out of the grave and sit on the grass, thanking his maker. They could not have known how he remembered being in his bed, very sick, and that then he remembered nothing until he woke up in blackness. They could not have realised that they were above his grave as it dawned on him, with absolute horror, what had happened, and that at that very moment he had wriggled his toe, tied to the bell on the gravestone outside, with all his might to raise the alarm.

Barker and Hill were long gone as he wept in the mud, thanking the Lord that the use of the bell, to alert a rescuer to individuals mistakenly buried alive, was now common practice, as the alternative was that his coffin would have become one of those bearing the marks of the inhabitant's terrified scratches in the inside of its lid.

"I can't believe someone heard!" he exclaimed in wonder, as the sky gradually grew lighter. "I didn't even have a chance to thank them."

A Gallery of Tigers

This has happened before, a long time ago, William remembered as he looked across the dusty attic. Until this moment, he had left that memory behind locked away in one of his 'boxes', chained, padlocked, stored in one of the recesses of his mind. This box had been marked 'do not open', long consigned to history, one of those childhood things which you convince yourself wasn't real and in the end, make a conscious choice to forget.

But here he was, looking out again, wondering what would happen now.

As a child, he had loved pictures as long as he could remember. Not for him the eddies and swirls of the sea; not the sand between his toes; not the high-pitched squeals of the playground. Behind heavy, drawn curtains all summer long, he would sequester himself in his father's study whenever he could. He would don the white, cotton gloves and climb the ladder to the top shelf, carefully removing each picture book in turn, handling the pages as if they were delicate eggs.

His father was a collector, a hoarder of rare books about art and he was quite well-known in the academic world. He gave long, dry lectures about the history of art to rooms full of young, keen students. He talked about symbolism and light and shade. He trawled with William in tow, through the dark corners of dusty bookshops, scouring the shelves to extract a rare gem. Other fathers went fishing or left William's young friends outside the pub with a shandy and a bag of crisps whilst they went inside, but not his father. William barely knew his father; they rarely spoke. He had the feeling that his father didn't really like children, that he was an inconvenience. He felt that his father had collected him in much the same way as he collected his books about art and that he was prized in much the same way with an air of ownership. When he did exchange words with him, it was often to shout at him to be quiet or to play somewhere else. So his heart swelled with joy when his father took him into his study one day to point out the vast collection that he must not touch. And so it was that as soon as he could, whenever his father was out of the house, William found himself poring over the priceless collection in his summer days of solitude.

Once, his father came back unexpectedly. William sensed him before he could see him but it was too late to hide, his father was in the room before he knew it. What happened next sat in William's head like a bad dream that does not leave you when you wake, distorted and shadowy and spectral; real but not real. His mother was in her studio, unaware and sleepwalking through her afternoon. William's father said nothing but he picked him up by the collar of his shirt and slung him over his shoulder. He thundered up the stairs with William, who was too afraid to shout out. His father threw him onto his bed where William landed, mute, like a sack. Then William's father removed his belt, pushed William onto his front and lashed him again and again until he drew blood and the sweat dripped down his forehead.

Downstairs, the afternoon passed as usual. A cool breeze fluttered through the house, lifting the curtains a little and his mother sipped at a large gin and tonic and lounged back in her chair, her lids closing slightly and the paintbrush slipping from her hand with a clatter to the floor.

When he had finished, William's father replaced his belt and fastened the metal buckle once more. "I am very tired," he said, "we shall not mention this again." And without another word, he left. William lay still, too afraid to move yet, the bedclothes still stuffed into his mouth. He felt like there were two Williams; one in his own body and one slightly outside his body looking in. He was still wearing the white cotton gloves. Even then though, in that moment, one of the Williams resolved that he would go back to the study again.

His mother was very different to his father but just as unreachable. She had very long hair with tiny braids woven into it and wore long fringed dresses that swept along the ground when she walked. In fact, she appeared to glide rather than walk. She was fey and spoke with a dreamy slur to her voice as if she were permanently sleepy. Her face was shiny and freckled like a girl much younger, and she was slight as if a breeze would whip her away. When she did pay him attention, it was with an overly eager manner with a wild and desperate edge to it. She held him too long and too tightly and her eyes always glittered with tears. She was often to be found in the large orangery, which she re-christened her 'studio'. This was littered with canvasses, tubes of paints and half-finished paintings. Occasionally, a nude model would be sitting there and would wink at William if he wandered in, looking for his mother. He would avert his eyes, red-faced, and mumble an excuse to leave. But his mother would rise and float over, fawning theatrically, kissing him and ruffling his hair and introducing him as her 'beautiful baby'. He would endure it, and then make his escape as soon as he could to the vast walled garden or back to his father's study if his father was away.

On one of these occasions, he happened upon a painting, reproduced on one of the pages, which had captivated him. It was a painting of a tiger, half-hidden by jungle leaves, standing and facing the viewer directly. He longed to touch its fur; bury his face deep into it and smell its warm, musty scent. The tiger from the painting stared out into his eyes, challenging but vulnerable. He felt it was facing down a predator larger than itself. He immediately connected with this tiger. It whispered to him from the page as it stood its ground, bravely facing its enemy with dignity. Every time he went to the study, he took the same book down and looked at the picture of the tiger in the painting.

Not long after, he had gone, bored, to wander around the huge national art gallery. It wasn't far from his home and in those days, even children his age could go out all day to play, not missed, returning home only for supper. He was luckier than most as his parents rarely missed his presence in the house. If he was outside at all, it was to wander the tangled jungle of the walled garden, in the grounds of their somewhat palatial home. To a child, perhaps this garden seemed bigger than it was and it offered a little bubble of the countryside, on the outskirts of the city. Still just under ten-years-old, no one worried if he rode the underground into a different kind of jungle with different kinds of walls, filled with sounds and crowds. Nobody even gave him a second glance as he slipped unnoticed through the crowds and into the entrance of the museum. It smelled of polish and antiquity as he made his way around. He sought the real painting of the tiger, knowing it was there, seeking an even more profound connection to it.

He heard the announcement half an hour before closing time, telling visitors to start making their way downstairs, and wondered if he had time to get up to the top floor. He decided to take the chance.

Mirrored walls surrounding the escalators reflected them back, giving the illusion that on one side the moving staircase ascended to the heavens, and that the other descended on infinitely, through the floor and down into the depths of hell. William watched multiple versions of himself ascending and disappearing as he journeyed up to the third floor.

And when he stepped off, he hurried through the maze-like corridors of the gallery floor until he reached room nine and straight away he knew it was the right one. There was the painting, the tiger staring benignly and poignantly out at him. Standing in front of it, alone in the room in the half-light, he met the tiger's eyes with his own. In his head, he heard a voice without words, in a language which was more a feeling than a language, but which he somehow understood, speak to him of bravery and defiance. In the distance of reality, he heard the bell ringing for the last call to empty the gallery before it closed. He turned to leave, but he was immediately surrounded by the thick foliage of the jungle and he looked out into the gallery through the tiger's eyes.

He felt himself inside the thick, coarse and shining pelt, smelled his own scent with a sense older than time. He thought as a tiger thought, without words but through instinct. He stood his ground for a moment, sensing his hunter to be near and then sped off into the undergrowth, stripes flashing through the greenery, flying through the jungle, faster than the wind.

When he stopped, feeling the danger vibrate through every sinew, he crouched low, his amber eyes with slit-like pupils, his body poised to pounce. He stalked, staying low, glimpses of orange and black occasionally flashing through, breaking his solid form to camouflage his body amongst the trees. He saw the hunter in a clearing, creeping along, rifle in hand, but with his back to him, lacking the tiger's keen sense of smell and sound. He pulled back on his haunches, about to spring upon the man, his claws out tearing into his back, ripping through flesh and muscle as his instinct to kill or be killed, to survive, took over. William's humanity was gone but what he had in its place was less destructive, yet more lethal. He imagined biting deep into the hunter's jugular, blood spewing out in crimson spurts. The man would fall; the tiger would fall upon him and feast.

But before he could pounce, William came again to human consciousness. He was lying on the wooden floor of the gallery, surrounded by people, with foamy spittle trickling from the corner of his mouth.

"Oh, thank God! He's alive!" said a stranger's voice with relief. "Thank God, I found him!"

The ambulance crew were doing checks that William was vaguely aware of, they had something around his arm and someone was holding his wrist. A soothing male voice was trying to reassure him.

"It's all right son, you fainted. We've got to take you to the hospital to be checked out because you have hit your head but it looks like you'll live. We've called your parents and your mum is going to meet us there."

"I was in the painting! I'm a tiger!" babbled William.

"OK lad. Try not to talk."

But as they carried him out on the stretcher, William heard one of them speaking with confusion.

"I can't understand how he got all those scratches and bruises. Can only think he must have had a fit or something."

William was in the hospital for two days; his mother stayed until the night time and left but his father did not come. They did lots of tests and concluded it was some sort of epileptic episode and 'childhood schizophrenia' was mentioned. But they were most worried about his tale of being the tiger. When he returned home, for months afterwards, William had to see a doctor once a week.

She wasn't like a proper doctor, in a white coat with a stethoscope; she was a doctor for the head. She talked to him a bit and he was encouraged to talk to her a lot. But William knew there were some things not to talk about. She wrote lots of notes about him and she had a file about him but eventually, the meetings stopped and William and his parents moved house from the outskirts of the city to the heart of the countryside. William thought he was saying goodbye to the old house and his old bedroom. He imagined leaving the other William behind in that room. But then his parents told him with a smile on their faces that they were keeping the old house and another family were going to take it over and pay them rent. It wasn't time to say goodbye to it forever.

The new house was, to William, like a mansion. It was a large old manor house, with an even bigger sprawling garden, and this house had a similar study to the previous one, like a library. Every wall was covered by books, with a ladder that slid along the shelves on runners, so you could reach the books at the top. William could continue with his secret exploration of his father's forbidden books, risking another beating worse than the odd clip around the ear or cuff of the leg for minor transgressions like playing too noisily; slightly thrilled by the danger of rebellion, the bravery of defiance. It had already been the worst, how could it be any more terrible?

One day, his parents, together, which was a rarity, took him to the circus. And that was where it happened, another memory that he had deliberately chosen to erase.

His father was more difficult than usual that day and more short-tempered and his mother even more sleepy and out of reach. They had bickered all day under their breath. It is so surprising that adults believe that their offspring cannot hear them, that there is an invisible wall around their conversations that a child cannot penetrate. But William knew there was something 'off' and felt too uncomfortable to enjoy the day. Quite apart from the fact that he hated the circus, hated the shabby, sad-looking animals, trained and whipped in the ring, who would return later to their cages, probably beaten again before moving on to the next town. But nobody had asked him if he liked the circus.

It was during the tiger's performance that it happened. After the lion was back in his cage, out came the tiger to the gasps of the crowd, softly padding along on his huge and lethal paws, his stripes rippling as he strode in powerfully. William watched the dignified beast, always his favourite creature, in his view humiliated by the lion-tamer, jumping up, rolling balls along, standing on a seesaw, all to the crack of the whip. William could no longer bear it; he pushed his way along the aisles of the seats and made his way out of the huge, big-top tent.

He sank down outside with his head between his knees, feeling as if he could not breathe, gasping to stop himself sobbing, silently shaking. He heard his parent's voices as if they were somewhere in the distance; they had followed him out and turned in the other direction once outside the tent. Their voices were raised against each other and although he could not hear the words they said, he felt the clash of two titanic forces, one roaring and vicious, and one defensive and slurring. He wanted it to stop.

As he rounded to the other side of the tent, he heard his father's attack.

"I never wanted the miserable little shit anyway! He's a pathetic, dreamy, sick and useless weirdo, just like his mother!"

His mother lunged out with a slapping motion and caught his father on the chin with her nails. Blood streamed down his chin.

For a second that seemed like forever, his father looked stunned. And then, with all his weight behind it, he punched his mother full in the face, spitting "Bitch!" as he did so. She fell backwards with the force, hands flying up to her face, which streamed with blood.

William froze and he saw his father freeze as they met, eye to eye. His father made a grab for him and wrenched him towards him by the arm. "Your mother's had an accident," he said, "she's hit her face. We need to go home."

"Yes sir," stuttered William. And then they were off, bundled into the car. William's arm was throbbing. When his father had grabbed him, he had heard a weird crunching noise and now his arm felt floppy and it burned with pain, but he bit his lip and screamed inwardly.

Back in the house, things seemed different. Nothing had changed or moved but the house had changed; it felt like when you came back from a holiday and everything was unfamiliar. Later, William would experience the same feeling upon returning from the hospital.

"We have to take him, Nicholas. We have to!" He heard his mother begging. She was cleaned up now, looking as if nothing much had happened except when you looked more closely for the bruise across her cheekbone, yellow bruising under her eye and a swollen nose, all covered with a layer of powdery make-up. They were arguing again about his arm. His mother said he had to go to the hospital and have an X-Ray because it might be broken or out of its socket. William pictured his arm dangling loosely, independent of his body, attached only by stretchy skin. His father didn't want him to go. He didn't like hospital, illness or injuries, and William hardly ever dared to cry if he was hurt as his father thought he should be a 'man'. But today it looked as if his mother would win as his father finally agreed that 'perhaps he should get it checked'.

The nurse asked William how it happened and William, glancing at his father and mother, repeated what he had been told. It seemed the nurse accepted the story and William himself almost believed that he had fallen down the stairs whilst playing with his mother. He was soon X-Rayed, treated and his broken arm put in plaster. But before he left, the doctor said that two ladies wanted to have a chat with him and then his parents.

They asked him all sorts of questions that seemed pointless. But William knew somehow that he should not tell them what actually happened. The trouble was William couldn't quite remember what he was supposed to say or what was real and he thought he might have got it wrong. The same ladies made him draw a picture of a house and he had to add a tree, and a snake, and a pond, which seemed pointless and confusing and he wasn't sure if he got it right. He put a tiger in it; it was standing like the one in the painting facing the snake, poised to attack it. He told the ladies he thought about making it bite the snake and lots of blood would come out, but then he changed his mind because the tiger was friendly really. They said his drawing was amazing but William knew that wasn't true because he knew paintings and his was not like those.

The same ladies had talked to his parents, separately. William didn't know what they said and if he had been in the room, he would have known that the ladies knew a lot about him already. They knew about the incident in the art gallery and that he had seen the man once a week. They knew that the family had moved from the city to the countryside and that William made up lots of odd stories. He would have seen his mother break down and tell them what had happened outside the tent at the circus and he would have heard her tell them that this had happened many times before. If he had been in the room with his father, he would have heard him tell them a lot of things about his mother too; how she hurt William on the stairs and neglected him, spending her days doped up on Valium and God knows what else, bringing nude people into the house on the pretext of painting them but that she was not a painter, she only thought she was.

After that, they had gone home and William had the strange feeling about home not being home once again. But the following week, the ladies came to the house again and this time they brought a man with them. The man looked like a fish with big, bulging eyes and he had a shark-like grin to match; a grin that didn't reach his eyes. When they left, they took William with them. William had put the memory of leaving into a box in his head like he had learned to do, but it had never really gone completely. Sometimes, through the years, he opened the box and he could still hear his mother's hysterical screams, smelling her fear somehow seeping through her pores as she tried to cling onto him, as he was pulled away by the man and carried off to the waiting car. His father was nowhere to be seen but William would see him a few weeks later when he went to live with him back in the house on the outskirts of the city. He was almost glad because he had spent the interim weeks in a small, smelly house, sharing a room with two grubby teenage kids, who hid his things and swore at him, calling him 'mental', and 'psycho'.

Those few weeks had given him another reason to be almost grateful to be back with his father in the old house. For all that he feared his father's anger on a daily basis, remembering the sting of the leather belt and the sear of the metal buckle splitting his flesh, at the small and smelly house, he had found out that things could be more terrible than the worst he thought he'd already experienced. They were worse than the worst when one of the other boys had climbed into his bunk with him and made him do things that he couldn't tell anyone ever. These things happened to the other William, not him. He fancied that he had left the other William behind in the little house, but secretly he knew that he had packed him in a box and brought him with him.

Nothing had changed in the old house, on the outskirts of the city. His father hired a woman to take care of him and he didn't see his mother anymore, not daring to ask why or where she was. He thought she must be dead; his father said she was 'dead to him'. He put her into a box in his head and closed the lid tightly. Her 'studio' was torn down and replaced by a proper room with brick walls and high windows. They were stained glass with biblical scenes on them, which made it look like a church. There was no light in the room anymore except for the muted, colourful, refracted glow, which penetrated through depictions of Mary Magdalene at Jesus' feet as he hung from the cross, or Judas spilling the salt at the last supper.

Because William and his father rarely crossed paths anymore, William was rarely in trouble and he grew more confident. He had a kindly tutor as well and William was sad to leave her behind to go to school, which his father had decided was best. He would be away for long, gruelling terms and not often allowed home for much of the holiday period as his father was away so much. Before he left though, William stole into the old study, filled once again with his father's books, the manor house with the huge library having been sold. He climbed to the top of the ladder, once again wearing white cotton gloves and he removed the book with the tiger painting in it and placed it carefully into his going away bag. The book was to stay with him for most of his school days and he would often take it out to look at it, hoping that he might once again become the tiger but knowing that he would not, as that was impossible and had never been real.

Time ticked away and William grew up. He made friends at school, struggled with maths, hated games, passed exams modestly, studied for and gained a degree in Art History. He did not forget about the book but he needed it less, eventually sneaking it back onto the bookshelves, where he felt it would be safer and his conscience no longer branded him a thief. The day he put it there was the day he left to go travelling, knowing that he would not come back to this place to live again. He traced the lines of the tiger painting once more, seeing an impossible glow from its serene shape on the page. He thought he glimpsed the other William, hiding in the shadows; he saw ghosts of himself everywhere – in the bedroom, or running through the walled garden. But these were transient wisps of the boy William, and they evaporated as suddenly as they appeared. He put the book back on the shelf and left for his new life.

William worked for a short time on a fruit picking farm in France. It was sweltering and exhausting work and there William had a brief but intense love affair with an English girl named Lia. She was difficult and demanding and came with a whole set of problems that awakened ghosts within William that he had kept dormant for many years. He knew what had drawn him to her, she reminded him of his mother, whom he realised was not dead, but was 'dead to him', as she had never come back to see him since the day he was taken from her. William was not close to his father; he had been afraid of him and sometimes he thought he hated him, but his mother hadn't come back and his father had stayed. Lia was fey and vulnerable looking like his mother, slightly unreachable and very cool. She wore round sunglasses over her pale green, cat-like eyes, and her sandy hair blew in the breeze as she lay back casually in the fields, making smoke rings with her cigarette. She had the same slight slur to her speech as he remembered in his mother; she always had a large glass of wine or spirit in one hand as she stirred chilli in a pan with the other. Lia liked to experiment with food or sex or drugs. She was a free spirit but she was a troubled one and after one too many nights of Lia drunkenly crying on his shoulder, and then raging at him, and scratching his face like a wild cat, William had to move on. He heard when he was much older that Lia had been married and had a child but that the child had been taken into care. He was not altogether surprised but it saddened him and made him shudder with a memory that crept through his soul like a ghoul.

The legacy she had left with William, though, was the seed of an idea. He thought about finding his mother. At first, he didn't do anything about it, it was just an idea. He travelled a little more and eventually, he headed back to England and took up a job as a curator in a museum in Edinburgh. And there he stayed until middle age, living his life with a reassuring routine, amongst dusty artefacts and paintings from the past, taking kids and parties on tours around the museum. He never married and rarely dated and could have become almost as dry and dusty as the museum pieces themselves but he was never dull, as his passion for the objects shone through and his enthusiasm infected all who heard him speak about them. He particularly brought the room containing the Victorian stuffed animals to life, making children giggle in delighted fear by roaring like the lions and tigers behind them. Some nights, when the museum was closed to the public, William would wander around that room and see their mighty shadows rise up, imagining them stalking their prey, moving magnificently through the jungle. In these quiet moments, William caught the thin spectre of a memory he could not clearly recall.

It was whilst in Edinburgh that he had heard about Lia from a friend of her brother's. Her brother happened to live there and had died unexpectedly and quite young. It was a gossipy tale and William hated to hear it but it reminded him again of how much she had resembled his mother. It felt odd that she might be here in Edinburgh for the funeral. So near but so out of reach. He began to understand why his mother might not have come back to see him. He thought of his father, with whom he now had little contact; of how he was still afraid of him and suddenly saw, with absolute clarity that she must have been afraid too, or maybe she had been kept away? He resolved to find her. But before he could even begin his search, a call came.

"William!" shouted his colleague, Peter. "There's a call coming through for you at the front desk!"

William took up the telephone.

"Is that Mr William Stratton? This is Penrose and Fountain Solicitors. I am calling on behalf of Mount Hill Hospital. I regret to inform you that your mother has died and you are her only known next of kin. We have a letter for you here."

The huge house on the outskirts of the city, where his father still lived, old and frail now but just as angry, the winking nudes, the soft slurred voice and the day he was wrenched away from her came flooding back like the lid had been knocked off a box and the contents spilt out messily. William's mind, assaulted by the unexpected like a hunted animal finally caught, went reeling. He managed to mumble a reply, and took down the address he needed to go to. He would not be able to find his mother now, never be able to ask her why she had not come back, never be able to blame her or forgive her or understand her point of view. Perhaps some answers would be in the letter?

When he arrived at the solicitors, a few of his questions were answered straight away. His mother had been living in an institution for the rest of her life; she had been diagnosed with multiple personality disorders and had spent much of her time medicated, only allowed out when accompanied. She always asked to go to the National Gallery and spent most of her time just sitting in front of a painting of a tiger at which she stared wordlessly fascinated until it was time to leave. The staff had spoken well of her as a woman who spoke little but often spoke of her son. Because he had not visited her, they imagined that he was one of her fantasies. They were devastated to find that he was real and regretted that he missed so much time with her. She had died, in fact, in front of that very painting, falling asleep and never waking up; they thought she had suffered a stroke.

William, alone later in his old room, in his father's house, tentatively opened the letter, and read:

'My Darling William, my son,

I am so sorry if I abandoned you. I don't want to blame your father, heaven knows, I spent most of the time in some sort of stupor trying not to 'see' him, trying to avoid what was happening. It was easier that way. I failed you, William but it was better not to notice things. Better for me and maybe, without me there, better for you too?

He put me here, in this place, saying things about me, and somehow, that was easier too. They have helped me here and have been kind to me. It was a comforting routine, not to see anyone, not to have to try anymore. And people noticed me here, in a good way. I could still paint pictures, and look at pictures, and no one could stop me. I got ill, William, and I think it was better for you not to see me.

But I wanted you to know one thing; I always believed what you said about the tiger. I tried often to get to the place you described, and I got close, William, I got so close!

The house was mine. Your father stole it when I was put in here but it was, and remains mine until I die, so if you are reading this, it is now yours.

I am so sorry,

I hope this helps to repair some of the damage done by the time we have lost, and that you have good memories of me.

Your loving mother always,
Natasha. X'

William felt, at first, angry. Angry that his mother was still so out of reach to him and that she didn't seem to know how much his loss of her had always shaped his life. Then he had more questions that would never be answered. This did not give him closure or relief but it brought fresh heartache and confusion. There was no real remorse; she seemed to have protected herself but could she really not have known about his father beating him? And what did she mean that she had always believed him? Tried to get there?

William sat on his bed for what seemed like an age, reluctantly accepting that this was now his own house but also knowing that his father was still there. It could be sold, of course, but where would his father go? He decided to let his father stay and stay silent about his ownership, at least until his father too was dead. He had his life and his work in

Scotland and he did not intend to return to this house of secrets and pain.

He wanted one thing from this house though, and he intended to find it. He went into his father's old study.

He had not been in there for many years and what he saw surprised him. Many of the books, especially the top shelves, were cleared of books. He supposed that now his father was in a wheelchair, he could no longer climb the ladder anyway. William took a deep breath and went into the sitting room at the far end of the house. There sat his father, bad-tempered and wizened. In a chair, yes, but still poised as if to lash out in anger, still terrifying. William swallowed the words of reproach that had formed in his head. His father, beater of women and children, liar, abuser of the vulnerable, and destroyer of love.

"Father, where did the books from the top shelf in your study go?" he finally asked.

"Too valuable to leave out anymore. I can't look at 'em, can I? No use for them now. They've been packed away. In the attic. But don't get any ideas in your head about stealing them again, I know you took one, not the most valuable one but I know. You can keep your hands off them, they go to the foundation when I've gone which won't be yet I can tell you. I've made a will, that's where they go. To experts, who'll appreciate them! Not grubby handed amateurs."

The same feelings that had always overcome William returned now. He was seized with the desire to take the books straight away, just as he had all those years ago, sneaking into his father's study and taking the book down to look at, risking a beating. He said nothing but left the room without a word, his knuckles white from the fists his hands had formed.

Later, William was in the attic. He turned over boxes, pushed away cobwebs which brushed across his cheek, and finally, he came upon it. The book he had always been obsessed with, the one with the painting of the tiger.

Eagerly but gently, he turned the pages, being sure to wear the white cotton gloves as in the habit of old. There it was, glowing from the pages, staring at him, looking right into his very soul, the tiger, beckoning him into the painting. And suddenly, there he was, looking out through the eyes of the creature, remembering this had all happened before in room nine, in the gallery all those years ago.

And he suddenly knew what would happen now. He turned and ran swiftly, elegantly, possessing strength and the wisdom of instinct. And as he reached the clearing, he crouched once more and began to stalk the hunter holding the rifle with his back towards him. He let the hunter turn and face him eye to eye; hunter and hunted; predator and prey. The eyes of the hunter were cold, with no compassion; filled with anger and an arrogant self-righteousness. William, as the tiger, sprang upon him and tore his throat out.

Downstairs, William's father called out for him, "Come back here! I know you are in that attic. Don't touch my books! I'll disinherit you, you little shit!"

His face grew red and then his words stuck in his mouth as he began to choke. His hands flew to his throat and he gasped for breath, beginning to turn blue. He slumped down in his wheelchair and onto the floor and finally, writhing in pain, he died, spittle drooling out of the corner of his mouth.

When they found him, no one could understand why he had choked or explain the mysterious scratches and wounds on his neck that resembled bite marks. Over the next few days, many people tried to contact William but no one could locate him.

William was exactly where he wanted to be.

Eternal Recurrence

Let me tell you how it is. This is the way the world is: we all live inside a giant dome and at night inside that dome, a heavy velour blanket lines the arch. Little stars are sewn on the inside and the malevolent moon really does have a face that watches us below. Our dome, once shaken, sends millions of fine glitter particles down from the sequin stars, showering us with the fall-out. Sometimes the pieces settle gracefully upon us like a halo, sometimes they fall beneath our feet, lost and crunched into eternal oblivion.

Mother smelled of warm straw. I breathed her in, taking her scent deep inside to freeze the moment. One day, Mother took a bath and never came downstairs again. "She is with God," said the lady as she led me from my world into 'care'. Trapped, unable to articulate it, I shook my fist at the sky. "I hate God," I said, though I was only repeating a new word. I didn't know what hate was and I imagined heaven was a white bandstand floating high above the clouds. How did all the people fit?

"Take that, you bastard," said my 26-year-old self, shaking my fist at the sky, as the clouds rolled in and the white flakes floated over the body of little Lilly, a few feet below the surface.

My earliest memory in my new home is of a svelte black cat. I remember her rasping tongue juxtaposed with her sensuous, velveteen coat. Years later, when I heard about a man in Africa whose arm was licked down to the bone by a lion while he slept, I recalled that tongue, a miniature version of the larger, more dangerous beast. I watched in fascination as she set upon her victim. The leather pads shot out spiteful knives to pierce and rip the flesh, jelly bursting from the wound like an over-ripe fruit. Those paws were wonderful weapons, cleaving fragile skulls. Inside the head of her prey was exquisite; a flower in bloom. There was less blood than I imagined; I wanted to know how all creatures bled when you cut them.

I considered: did a cat always land on its feet when you threw it from a top floor window? How long could an animal live without food? There seemed only one way to find out. The cat went missing. Whilst nobody heard her desperate, whining mewls, it seemed she ceased to exist. I went every day to monitor my experiment.

In the playground, I'd earned minus points. My politeness; my tangled feet; my lack of team effort. I stood at the edge, watching, waiting. I was an observer of aliens, stupid-featured people who waddled in my way. I studied them, recognising their inferiority. I eavesdropped, longed to be them, but I despised them.

As I lit the fire around the cat's body, I was seduced; I wanted to lick the flames. I tried to see dancing figures, searched for faces of the dead but instead I saw my own face reflected, returning the eyes of a creature like Frankenstein's, bound to solitude. I learned not to fear but to create fear; I grew powerful. They knew which hand ignited that tiny funeral pyre but they could not prove it.

A voracious reader, I devoured knowledge whole with the Python's avarice. Biding my time, my experiments grew daring. In failing light one summer, a small runt played my game. Tied to a tree, his face blanched to waxy pallor. Fear reduced his features to a mask. Reality was suspended and I observed. How long would it take for him to succumb? Weak overpowered by strong, this is the rule of the game. Such was my power that I relinquished it, untied the ligatures, and released him. He left confused, grateful and beholden, owing me his life.

I took myself to the limits but never crossed the final boundary; the line drawn because of my connection to this suffocating, limiting existence. I needed to free myself; I needed to reaffirm my conviction. 'There are always two', the voices echoed, 'a master and a servant'.

Sarah had Willowy limbs and black hair with a childish, sporty build and always seemed a little lost. Her face wore a hooded appearance at times, the eyes remained impassive. If there was inner turmoil, it remained hidden. It was the trait that drew me to her, mirroring my talent for secrecy. I hid behind a veneer of tranquillity; I sensed a soulmate. I knew she recognised the same in me, and so was a suitable lieutenant. I could expound on my theories and I had someone to chart my progress. She was a curator of my books and journals and I groomed her for her role. Like the proverbial falling tree in the forest, did anything exist without a witness? My genius required an audience to make it real.

Sarah brought him to me the first time I saw it through. A young man she had shared a drink and confidences with. I don't know what I intended until the moment arrived but I had to prove myself. Limits only exist in the mind. Forget limitations, make your own morality, and liberate free will. Sarah lapped up these words as if they were from a prophet. That day she wore a coral choker that seemed to slice her neck neatly in two, anaemic beads of blood from her beheading shining liquidly against the waxen flesh.

He was laughing 'pleased to meet you' when I twisted the knife deep into the sinewy neck, almost severing the spinal cord. His eyes rolled back in his head as the blood curdled and foamed from his mouth. He spasmed violently and uncontrollably, beginning the macabre dance as he staggered back like a half-living rag doll, his final gasp mimicking the sound of water being sucked into a drain. I found the answer that all creatures bleed differently when you cut them.

What physical and mental sensations occurred as this happened? My heart thumped so hard I thought it would leap from my chest and lay pulsating on the floor. An icy arrow lurched at the speed of sound through my veins. The power and the glory. God was dead. He did not stop me. The pathetic police search unearthed nothing. I even helped them, expressing my concern, the art of which I had practised in the mirror until I believed it. I could sense, however, that Sarah wanted more. The bed loomed between us like a vast, chaste canyon. So, I gave her what I could. I gave her Lilly.

When little Lilly awoke in her comfortable home that crisp morning, it was snowing. The first thing she did was to look out of the window of the small, terraced house; she saw a magpie. To Lilly, it was a portent of doom. She chanted the mantra that was so entrenched in her. "Good morning, Mr

Magpie, I hope you and your family are well." It would be safe now.

The heavy sky gathered over the hills that bright morning. It cracked; more snow fell softly, creating eerie muffling. Snow collected on Lilly's coat and nestled on her eyebrows. Fresh, untrodden snow has purity until it becomes unhallowed grey slush. The cold bit the young girl's fingers and nipped at her cheeks; blood hurried away from the surface, giving her the complexion of a porcelain doll. Then, through snow's shroud, she saw Sarah, the car door open invitingly. "Need a lift, Lilly?" Sarah asked casually. "Weather's suddenly turned, hasn't it?"

Black and white smile-to-smile eight-millimetre grainy flicker. A plea, a scream, she has her 15 minutes of fame. The celluloid legacy of Lilly, now beneath the snow, those images retrieved which finally betrayed me.

Sarah led them to their discovery. She wore shame beneath the mask of deception, a Chinese box of encased emotions. A careless name scribbled on a notepad. An ill-placed photograph marking the place in a romantic novel.

At 5 am, a furious commotion woke us. The door was blasted off its hinges by hob-nail boots. A cacophony of shouting wrenched us from our beds. Identify this, identify that. "Yes," I told them, "I recognise that. Yes, I do know that girl in the photograph. Yes, I took it." They tornadoed through my possessions and journals... two ignorant words: 'sick pornography'.

In the midst of chaos, Sarah took flight. She slipped from my grasp onto the street. I heard the screech of inevitability and the second commotion of the morning led to Sarah, lying in the road, a snow angel, blood fanning from her sides like wings, her choker broken and the coral beads scattered on the tarmac. She was still breathing.

Sarah was vilified and renounced her faith in me, turning to another, more palatable one, a higher power, cynically working her ticket to freedom. I graciously accepted my fate, glancing heavenwards to the only piece of sky I was to see for many years. But rage still burned brightly, gaining deeper intensity over time.

They keep coming to the white room containing a table, myself and the person opposite. They're trying to unearth more buried secrets, exhume them from my mind's makeshift grave. They seek the truth but as I point out, truth is only another viewpoint and can divide into a prism of refracted alternatives.

I have Zapruder-thoughts; silent cine-flickers frame-by-frame. I had a dream once. I dreamed of the sandman climbing a telegraph pole with a sack full of sand, me in my cot-barred prison. I want to sleep before he comes. He only does his job but I don't like him. I know he loves his work. Back, back, back they take me. Everything has happened before and none of this has happened yet.

But look. Here is my mother and she is holding a bottle labelled 'Dr Patternson's famous pills – for irregularities of every description'. She examines the medicine. The wind blows, the clouds scud by, the world turns, the moon rises and the sun sets a thousand times. My existence hangs in the balance. She puts it down again and makes her decision. I will be born.

A tiny speck of glittering dust drifts down from above and settles.

Outside the Window

Usually, at this time of night, there was a lot more activity. It was too quiet. Something felt wrong.

I hoisted myself reluctantly out of the cosy chair, into which I had sunk, curled up with a blanket and shuffled over to the window. For some reason, I felt as if I shouldn't draw attention to myself, an irrational feeling, yes but causing me to gently tweak the curtain aside very slightly, to allow a view of the street below with minimal movement.

I smiled to myself. The irrationality of my fear seemed to be confirmed, the street was empty and nothing seemed out of the ordinary. But still, the feeling persisted. Wasn't it too empty? Shouldn't Mrs Adler across the street have been putting the bins out for the following day?

Didn't that little family usually take a late evening stroll, trying to settle the kid in the pushchair because clearly she never slept? I'd noticed the mum before, frazzled with dark circles under her eyes. Sometimes the couple were rowing under their breath, with an older child following them, scuffing his feet. He must have been around 12, at that point when they develop a surly expression and pretend they aren't with the parents. In his case, I could quite understand it.

There was always a lot of movement out in my street. Sometimes, even after the streetlights had gone out, you could hear footsteps echoing on the pavement, voices muttering, and the occasional car. But not tonight.

I returned to my chair, sat on the edge of it, tapping my toes on the rug. Nothing to worry about, surely? It was ridiculous to feel so uneasy. I was probably just anxious because I'd dozed off a bit. Last night, I'd woken in a sweat, dreaming about Vikings, of all things. My lurid imagination can be overactive at times. I started to relax a little. I knew what to do to feel a little calmer; I'd make myself a drink, have a piece of toast and put the telly on. That always worked. It keeps you company if you feel unsettled, the television, puts things back into perspective, like you are reconnected to the world.

I slipped a light cardigan on as it was distinctly chillier than it had been earlier and shuffled off into my tiny kitchen. But even the sound of the tap running, the kettle boiling and the grill pan clanging, sounded abominable in the silence that seemed to hang in the air.

I put my head back around the doorway into my living room. I had that peculiar feeling that someone was sitting there watching me. You know, that feeling when you feel someone behind you and it creeps up your neck, daring you to turn around? But no, I was still alone. I tentatively entered the room and crossed once more to the window. I peered out into the dimly lit street once again. Nothing. For a moment, I was transfixed by the stillness, the emptiness. It was unnatural; it was like the world had stopped. It must have been only a minute, and then I was brutally shaken from my reverie by the screaming smoke alarm.

I rushed back to the kitchen with my heart pounding at my ribs.

"Dammit!" I cursed.

I grasped the grill pan in a panic, dropping it and the charcoaled toast to the floor with a yelp as the hot tray caught my arm. I grabbed the broom and began to whack the alarm in temper. Who would put the thing in a kitchen, of all places?

As I nursed the pink welts on my arm, it struck me that when my inattentiveness had precipitated such an event before, the neighbour from across the hall had always come running, knocking to check I wasn't about to burn down the building. I braced myself but no one came.

It was odd, I thought. But still, I started again with the toast, this time keeping a watchful eye on it until finally, I settled in front of the television, once more tucked under my blanket.

The television didn't work. The screen was as silent as the street, black on every channel. I kept switching frantically in my impatience. I reset the Sky box. But still nothing happened.

"Oh, for God's sake!" I said out loud to no one.

I turned it off altogether and picked up the book I had been reading before I dozed off earlier. But I just could not settle, so I decided to go for a walk.

Outside, there was definitely something missing but I couldn't decide what it was. No matter. I was wrapped up warmly in my coat and hat and I took up a brisk pace. It felt energising as I breathed in the cold night air and I felt my muscles wake up as I moved. The street glittered with small pools of reflected artificial light and there was a fine mist in the air. The season was just beginning to change and the day had been warm but the nights had still to catch up, the insistent breeze nipping at my cheeks. However, I walked on, feeling much happier.

But before long, I began to feel uneasy again. Although the street was lit, every house I passed was in darkness, every shop, every corner café closed. As I rounded the corner to the marketplace, all of the stalls, as was usual at this time, sat deserted and empty, signalling no clue to the vibrant bustle of activity, life and colour they had embodied a few hours earlier. But tonight, their abandonment was even more eerie. Gone were the colourful coverings, the wares displayed like candy. All that remained were flapping posters, adrift from their fixings, as the wind whistled in between the stark, bare legs of the stalls.

Darkness pervaded, stalking along each orderly row of skeletal structures, punctuated here and there by watery beams of light. Yet there were corners which were so solidly black, that a fanciful mind could shape-shift sinister scenarios of silent shadows whispering and gliding insidiously from them while your back was turned.

In the street, night had drawn a darker veil over the landscape suddenly and precipitately, taking me unawares. It is peculiar how such an ordinary area by day, can take on such a sinister and threatening undertone when shrouded in black silence with only the merest glimpse of a pale moon peeping between the houses, and an endless black street. In the moon's diluted gaze, puddles occasionally twinkled. It was impossible to see any stars, and if there were any living creatures about, other than myself, they gave no sign of their presence. All was silent and still.

Beginning to feel even more unnerved, I headed for the square, where I thought I might hope to see signs of nightlife cranking into gear. I wasn't one for a late night out on the town these days but the thought of some movement, any movement, was comforting right now, in this twilight world. But when I arrived, comfort was in short supply, for the sight I beheld was yet another dark and deserted scene. Where only yesterday, lurid lights on tempting signs blinked and beckoned the partygoer into various establishments, the sound of music's pulsating beat throbbing and spilling out onto the street, again there was nothing. No sound, no laughter, not a single solitary footstep.

For no logical reason, I quickened my pace, breaking out finally into a trot. Desperately, I scanned the streets for signs of life and as I did so, I was aware of the streetlights being snuffed out, one after another, along their rows, as if an almighty being was blowing out the candles on his giant birthday cake, one by one. Closer and closer came the approaching darkness, and I began to run, stumbling as I did so, feeling all the time as if the shadows were in pursuit of me and fearing that something terrible had happened. I headed in the direction of the one place where I felt assured I might find another living soul: the hospital.

Turning off the ever-darkening street, I came upon the supermarket. I paused for a moment, mesmerised by what I saw: trolleys stood empty and abandoned; parking bays were scattered with empty cars; receipts and even a couple of £5 notes tumbled randomly across the tarmac, seemingly the last vestiges of paper that controls our lives. I shook myself out of my trance and ran on. Up this street, down that road, nothing and nobody anywhere to be seen, even the moonlight appeared to have been snuffed out. At last, I arrived at my destination.

The car park here was similarly deserted. Disturbingly, cars seemed to be strewn about in disarray, doors hanging open as if their occupants had left them in a hurry and never returned. I reached into my pocket; I had remembered to pick up my phone! I tried to dial out to someone, anyone in my contacts but there was no signal, only a blank screen. I made for the hospital entrance.

Bursting through the double doors, I found myself greeted with the same eerie silence that seemed to pervade the whole of the town. Perhaps it was the same in other towns, I thought, with mounting terror. Empty trolleys were strewn about the corridors, empty beds and wards. It seemed as if the whole population had simply disappeared.

Now, the full horror of the situation took hold of me, as I ran through the building shouting and crying, screaming and calling, hoping for any response. And then I saw it. I heard something that sounded like a human voice, a strangled cry for help. I turned and I saw the figure of a woman, hunched in a corner, reaching out towards me in a silent scream as a creeping black shadow grew long across the floor and she was devoured by its darkness.

Blindly, I turned on my heels and ran; back through the building, banging into walls and falling over upturned trolleys, not stopping until I was outside and not even then. I ran and ran without looking back until at last, I was back in my room crouching under the window, jabbing at my phone in futile despair with no streetlight shining through the gloom to comfort me and not a single sound to be heard. It was then that I realised what I had found so odd when I had first stepped outside. There was no birdsong, and no birds.

****

Three weeks have passed and I am still here in my room peering occasionally out of the window, wondering when it will be my turn to be taken, enduring the endless uncertainty of my dwindling existence, with only the certainty of being the last forgotten person, perhaps on the whole planet, to be left alive and alone.

The End of the Beginning

When the call came, it was in the early hours, entirely unexpected and absolutely unwelcome. Lia, sprawled precariously on the edge of her drab and dusty sofa, rolled herself languidly onto the floor and felt around for the incessantly ringing phone.

As usual, her phone was somewhere on the floor, under the piles of cigarette packets, papers and empty cans which littered the threadbare carpet. It chimed, hysterically, with the ringtone her son had set for her last time she had seen him. Finally, she located it between a stale coffee cup and a piece of foil. She squinted at it, just making out a blurry 'no caller id' and the time, 3 am. She swore as she slid her thumb across it.

"Hello," she croaked, surprised at her own voice, which, annoyingly, did not seem to be functioning. The line crackled a little.

"Hello!" she ventured again, this time sounding a little more human but possibly slightly explosive in the effort to override the throaty creak.

"Hi Lia, it's me," said an uncertain voice at the other end.

Lia thought that they might have to give her a bit more of a clue.

"Lia, it's Jo," said the caller, obviously guessing her predicament.

"Jo," creaked Lia, "it's 3 am."

Lia instinctively began to gather up piles of debris, suddenly anticipating her sister appearing on her doorstep.

"Lia, I have some news," said Jo, tentatively.

"Jo, where are you?" Lia asked abruptly.

"Lia, I'm in Edinburgh," replied Jo, impatiently, "the signal's not great and this isn't my phone. Look, Lia? I'm at Peter's house. Lia? Oh God, Look…he's dead."

As soon as Lia had heard the word, 'Edinburgh', her insides had contorted. After that, she had only heard the word 'dead'.

Jo twittered on, and Lia heard the words 'mum' and 'arrangements' but she was still stuck on 'dead'. It was as if a spiny hand had reached up from below and pulled her, hurtling down a spiralling alternate reality, where everything she knew hung surreally above her, carrying on in its parallel realm, while hers was irrevocably changed.

When the call ended, Lia realised she had forgotten to ask how her brother had died. She wasn't sure about anything right now, except that she had a pounding hangover and her muscles ached all over. So, the first thing she needed to do was remedy these two afflictions. She reached for a can of cider and began to prepare a fix of her drug.

This morning routine was reassuring. She prepared the drug lovingly, with attention to detail. After all, it was her most reliable and long-lasting relationship. There was a boy once, years ago in France. William. Obsessed with paintings. They had picked fruit together and been inseparable for one summer. Somehow they understood each other. But it would

104

never have lasted. Lia knew, without William saying a word, that he was as needy and screwed up as she was. She let him go before any more damage was done. Now her fingers accidentally brushed the delicate needle as she adjusted the fine point, and it sent a glorious shiver down her spine. Minutes later, she began to drift into peace, the edges of reality blunted, almost as soon as the blood cloud mushroomed into the barrel after she had plunged the point home. All life distilled into this perfect moment as she receded quietly into herself.

A few days later, she stood in a funeral parlour in Edinburgh, preparing to say her farewells to her brother, Peter. She liked the city. It had beauty and also hard edges. She understood why he had lived there, why he had never come back. She had already spoken to his wife, whom she barely knew; a delicate and twittering woman, always nervous and subdued, as if she had to apologise for existing, but beautiful, like a china doll. And she had managed to be sober in front of his children: sweet, adorable children, so sad-faced, with large vulnerable looking expressions in their eyes, like Victorian orphans. Lia had managed to hold a reasonable conversation with her sister, and had made arrangements for their mother's arrival. Now her thoughts turned to that imminent arrival.

Lia had not spoken to her mother for quite some time. Not since they took her son away, three years previously, in fact. She winced as she anticipated the cold and civil, judgemental tones with which her mother would greet her. Perhaps she would ignore Lia altogether, which would be infinitely preferable, she thought. She recalled the look of disgust, which her mother took no pains to hide, whenever she looked at her. With horror, Lia suddenly realised that there would be a wake! She began furiously calculating how much time she could spend in the bathroom without being missed at this 'after-show' event.

Now, like her mother and sister, she had come to see Peter and say goodbye. She had no idea what she was going to do or say since she had not been alone with him for over 20 years. She felt the familiar churning in her gut. She knew he'd be in a coffin but what could she expect to see? She had that feeling of danger again, rising up inside her permanently twisted gut. Why had she even come here, so unsure she could do this? They were all going in, one by one. All she had to do was decline, but something in Lia always drew her down this road. Again and again, like a blow constantly hitting a bruise.

The room was hushed and peaceful, with dimmed lighting, flickering fake candles and filled with the heady scent of lilies. This wasn't his final resting place, Lia reflected but it was the last time she'd see him, before they took him away; before they burned him.

She peeped at him like a nervous child. There he was, looking as if he were sleeping. Calm. No horror or panic written on his face to reveal his encounter with death; his eyes were shut. Even fine lines seemed to have melted away and the story of his life's endeavours was not written in his expression. There was no sign of a struggle or unwillingness to leave this world, no sign of regret or remorse, no final confession on his lips. He was greyer but relatively unchanged and simply at peace. Lia half-expected him to sit up, grinning maniacally like he had done as a teenager and declare "only joking!" He was always a bit of a joker; it was a laugh a minute with Peter.

Lia began to shake uncontrollably, then suddenly, violently, rage flooded in like a tsunami and she imagined herself pounding on the coffin with her fists until it shattered into a million pieces. She looked down at her hands. She had been picking at her thumbs, tearing at the quicks until they bled.

She thought about when she was seven and he was 14, when he had climbed into her bed with his sweaty, hairy body, smelling of Lynx. She thought about when he had touched her, telling her it was just a game, putting his hot hand over her mouth. "Ssh! Don't tell! It's our secret special game." She thought about Jo, who was older, who had not believed her when she told her later. Jo, who had moved out and abandoned her. Her mind turned to her mother, who should have known, who must have known and yet who had chosen to remain in sweet, silent ignorance, failing as surely as Lia had failed her own son.

Her son. She had trained herself not to think of him. Of course, she always thought of him when she was strung out; she could not stop her mind flying to him straight away. And she could only see him when she was strung out, was never drunk or high when she was with him. They had only just allowed her to have unsupervised visits, she couldn't risk losing that or worse, losing him forever to a distant new family like they had threatened once before. His father was long gone, inconsequential; the kind of man who would give you a black eye if you smiled at another man in the wrong way, or for putting on a pound in weight. And then she fleetingly remembered her own father. Weak, arrogant, distant and then finally gone for good, leaving Peter to be the man of the house.

Lia sank to the floor. God, she needed a drink and a hit. She instinctively reached for the drugs in her coat pocket and felt reassured. Not long now before she could slip away. She felt strangely disembodied again as if she didn't quite recognise herself. She would hardly be able to trust herself to speak, as she knew she would find it difficult to recognise the sound of her own voice. Therapy had called it 'depersonalisation'. Therapy didn't cure her of it though. What was the point of giving something a name if you didn't cure it?

Just then, a harsh shaft of light penetrated the room. It invaded the corners, exposing the artificial candles as cold parodies of real flames. Words from Shakespeare floated incongruously into her brain; a line about the stars putting Juliet's cheek to shame. It would surprise most people that she'd liked Shakespeare at school and could recite long passages of his words. She had not thought about that for years. Oddly, a small smile began to play around her lips. She was exhausted and broken but at the same time, strangely lighter. The situation was absurd; she was beside her dead brother, following his sudden and tragic loss at a relatively young age and here she was feeling like she might begin to break into wild laughter. An absurdly pompous voice in her head played out the obituary: *he leaves behind him a grieving widow, and young family, a doting mother and two adoring sisters, from whom he has been so prematurely taken.* Now she did begin to shake with black, stifled laughter, and slid down into an hysterical heap. Thinking that anyone who entered would assume she was overcome with grief only served to increase her amusement. It seemed like quite some time before she finally peeled herself up from the floor, barely comprehending it all.

At the door, she paused briefly, glancing a final time at the lifeless body in the wooden box, then she left the room and began the long walk down the dim corridor hoping she could find her way back.

The Morning

The morning brings silence. The house is forlorn, still sweating in its charred remains; burnt-out insides blackened, stripped and gutted. Charcoal-covered chairs lay strewn about, their legs crisped to a cindery twig; sharp stakes to pierce the heart. Silvery objects now darken; their reflective surfaces no longer polished, but warped, distorting any shapes they mirror. Cutlery still set out on the table seems to anticipate the return of the family; go upstairs and you will see rows of ragged clothes half-hung in the remains of once-white wardrobes.

A girl enters unnoticed. The house does not pay much attention to her. She moves softly, observing the scene. She touches the crisp, ash-coated chairs, running her delicate, white fingers over their splintery surface. You see her take her place at the table, eyeing the bowls – this one is too small; this one too large; this one is just right. Holding the melted spoon up to the shaft of light that shoots across the room, sprinklings of particles twinkling and falling down its beam, she examines it for her own reflection. There is no reflection; only a memory.

Her memory takes her to the foot of the stairs. She treads carefully, crunching the last of their destroyed possessions underfoot as she ascends. She tries each soiled and damaged bed – this too hard; this too soft; this just right – and wearily lays her head to rest.

Where are her family? The ones who filled the spaces at the table, who filled the rows of clothes that waited on their ash-coated hangers? The flickering film re-winds and takes her to a beach, where seagulls cry as the white dunes echo with the sounds of children.

The angry fire had raged and raged. Like a beautiful beast, it swept through the house, licking its way over the contents with its glowing tongue. Softly it whispered, seductively gliding gently, devouring anything in its path with unapologetic glee. Its bright Autumn colours jealously turned the house to the black of the night and, stealing a glance in the mirror, it cried with triumph, "I am the fairest of them all." The fire blazed all night, consuming the house, obliterating traces of existence; it felt unstoppable, but its rage could not last forever and eventually, it fizzled out and fell quiet.

In the burned remains, the girl rises from the ashes and spreads her cindery wings. Now the house protests at her audacity, that anything could come from this destruction. The clock still ticks time on the charred mantlepiece, loudly chiming its insistence to be heard. This clock is now irrelevant; it charts time's march for no reason; it chimes for no-one. Two more clocks, one in the hall and one in the living room, tick un-synchronised, out of step. The day-to-day routines continue: the oven timer bleeps, the dishwasher beeps; the central heating roars into life, despite the buckled windows no longer containing any warmth. And outside, machines grind on, functioning and fit for purpose. But they are no longer needed.

A thousand glacial winds have come and gone, blown through the hapless planet with no inhabitants: a global empty room. Entire galaxies and a million stars have been born, withered and died; time's celestial calendar moves on with no-one to change the dates. The universe is a Russian doll full of emptiness and this house is not the key, it is the speck of dust on a rusty lock.

She rises to search again. Each memory is magnified, a fragment of her former self, which has splintered and twisted into sounds she cannot identify in this new incarnation. She does not know where she is, or what she is, yet she knows where she came from. You could watch her, if you could see her, brush down her charred and sinewy arms which are scarred with truth.

She herself is only a memory, a shadow. She sweeps cinders silently, rakes the ashes of the dead fireplace. She does not know why she must rake those ashes, but she must; each dead splinter brings fresh pain and though the fire does not re-kindle, it lies dormant, like a mythical creature longing for awakening. With delicate fingers, she feels the fabric of the hanging clothes, tracing the outline of the forms they fitted, sensing the imprint of their missing owners.

The search may be fruitless and without end, yet while it continues, there is hope. The warped reflections and whispering silhouettes circle, wraith-like, branding her with their insistence. They beg to re-claim this revenant from obscurity; persistent fingers push her to take tentative steps into light, where outside provides an arid wilderness of limitless infinity, waiting for the resurgence of one flower.

The Crack in the Lens

When I awoke, I peered cautiously out from behind my lashes and hair; hair which was strewn in tendrils across my face.

The blackness was at first impenetrable, pierced only by a single shaft of early dawn sunlight, dust motes floating like ground diamonds along the shard. We are all dust, twinkling along our various pathways, ready to settle and finally disintegrate into nothing.

Gradually, I began to make out my surroundings. Bare floorboards splintered in my hands as I traced them with my fingertips, running my nails into the crevices, collecting the stickiness of unnamed substances which had formed there over the years. I could just make out shabby, flowered wallpaper that peeled, hanging in strips. Vast swathes of holey, moth-plundered curtains billowed in a slight draught, which whistled in from the star-shaped cracks in the sashed windows.

I tried to lift my head but could barely raise it off the floorboards. It felt as if my whole body had been run over by a steam roller, blending me in so completely with my surroundings that where the floor ended and I began was indecipherable. I trawled through my tangled brain for any clue to explain my whereabouts and predicament but I found nothing to enlighten me. Now I began to feel panic rising. My mind never fails me; my retention of detail is extraordinary. Why could I locate nothing to prompt a memory?

I groaned as the dull ache spread throughout my body. Somehow, I battled through the discomfort and managed to half-prop myself up upon my elbows, albeit barely raised from the floor. I took in the surrounding scene once more as my eyes began to adjust to the dim light but could discern nothing particularly unusual about the shabbiness of a run-down building, save the peculiarity of the situation itself.

Under such intense pressure, I might reasonably be expected to throw myself into a blind panic and yet here I was, trying very rationally to ascertain the circumstances which had brought me to the floor of this dingy attic. Indeed, it was not the situation that set my heart racing, but the fact that I could not remember how I had ended up there. Even then, I was annoyed rather than troubled by this.

As I began to regain some movement, I knew that I should attempt to get out. Gingerly, and with some pain now as my limbs returned to life, I clawed myself to my feet. To my right was a small window and I limped over to it. As I drew aside the wretched excuse for a curtain, I was, for the first time, aware of more than a dull ache at the back of my head and across my chest. I put my hand to the back of my head at the same time as I felt a warm liquid trickle between my fingers. Now it finally dawned on me why I could not remember the events of the previous hours. Something had struck the back of my head and the blow had been enough to draw blood and cause amnesia. My hackles rose in anger and fear. I knew now that I must certainly escape from that room and whoever or whatever, had put me there.

I peered once more out of the ever-lightening window. The garden was in a similar state of disrepair to the room. There was no furniture in the room but there was a good deal of it lying discarded in the garden. The grass was tall and the weeds overgrown. Broken glass adorned the unruly spectacle. Clearly, the path to freedom would not be easily negotiated via this exit.

My eyes finally fixed upon the door but I held out little hope of it yielding easily. I tried the handle but I was correct in my assumption, it was locked or stuck fast. With regret, I turned my attention back to the window, knowing that this was my only way out and resigning myself to the cuts and bruises that would inevitably follow.

I covered any bare flesh on my arms and hands with my coat and slammed my fist into the window as hard as I could. The brittle old glass shattered and I kicked out the remaining teeth-like strands to allow myself to climb through.

The window was higher up than I anticipated and I swore as I swung down and landed awkwardly. Almost instantly, I was aware of a creeping sensation of being watched. A low rumbling sound began and my head snapped around. Two yellow eyes pierced the mist in the murky dawn. Like a stand-off, the creature and I eyed one another and I realised I had to make a split-second decision. Adrenalin numbed the pain of movement as I whirled around, sprang to my feet and bolted for the fence and gate. As I began to climb, I spotted another pair of savage, drooling jaws approaching. The two dogs snapped at my heels and I just managed to evade them as I swung up and over the fence, missing my footing at the top and landing unceremoniously on the concrete on the other side.

I was in a dimly lit alleyway, which at night, would have conjured fanciful imaginings of Jack the Ripper approaching with his blade. A genuine Victorian street lamp hung above, albeit the gas light was long replaced by a light bulb. In the early dawn, with the threads of sunlight breaking up the gloom, the alleyway was, nevertheless, very uninviting and the dogs growled ominously on the other side of the fence.

I had no choice. I had to go through the alley. Logically, there was little chance of anything untoward happening there, unless the dogs had alerted their owner, who presumably was the person who had put me in the room. I moved as fast as I could with my injuries.

Dripping blood from the arm where some of the glass had caught me, limping slightly and with a definite awareness of my blood trickling into the hair at the back of my head, I made my way towards the next street light at the end of the alleyway, which was shrouded in the morning mist. Spider webs, beaded with dew, hung about like gothic lace; beautiful traps for the unsuspecting fly. Bits of broken web tickled my face and stuck to my lips and I brushed them aside.

No memory of why I was in the room or how it happened, had returned to me yet but as I entered the quiet street as the town began to wake up, vague visual flashes re-surfaced in my mind; a bar, coloured lights, noise, loud music and a vague sense that I had not been my real self. I could see in my head, a man and a woman across the bar talking heatedly and then leaving. I knew that I had followed them. But I had no idea why.

I had not forgotten who I was. It was only details of the situation that would not come to me. I wasn't sure where I was but I only had to hail a cab and I could return home. I felt for my phone. It was in my pocket but it was dead. I listened carefully and I followed in the direction of noises which would certainly lead me to the main street.

"13 Friday Street, please," I instructed the driver, aware that I must have looked like a wreck.

Soon, I was back in my house and the first thing I did was check every door and window for signs of forced entry. There were none. Steeling myself, I headed for the bathroom mirror for vanity would not permit me to ignore possible damage to my face. The sight which greeted me revealed that I was surprisingly unscathed. A few scratches on the cheeks and forehead, a cut arm, of course and bloody, matted hair. Some of my clothing was torn but this evidenced only signs of a moderate struggle, presumably before I had headed for oblivion in the dusty attic or maybe even before I got there. But the most telling sign staring me in the face to explain the memory blackout more than the blow to the skull, was the enormous dilation of my pupils.

"Aah!" I exclaimed. "That explains it. I was drugged."

I feared now that the memory might never fully return but I hoped that I might retrieve enough information to understand what had happened. I fleetingly pictured again the face of the woman from the bar in my mind's eye, as she left. She wasn't distressed and I knew her. Two valuable pieces of information; I searched my neck and arms for puncture wounds. There were a few old scars, but nothing new. Finally, there it was in the side of the neck. They, whoever they were, had obviously shot the drug in there and made sure with a final blow to the head. I decided to find out what they had given me so that I would have a clearer idea of when or if, any details might return. There was one person who was best qualified to help me with that information and that person was K, who would be at the hospital, as usual. He name was Kiaron Reeves, but I had known him as K since we were small. Before I left my home, I put my phone on charge.

"Midazolam," said K, "and what the hell have you done now? You look like you've fallen through a window!"

"I have, in a manner of speaking. More accurately, I threw myself through it to get out of a room I didn't want to be in. I don't have time to explain, in fact, I can't remember it all yet and what I need to know is, am I likely to?"

"No. Not this time." He replied. "Look," he sighed, "I am giving you no more information until you tell me what you've been up to. I am your oldest friend, and probably your only real friend. I need to know or if anything happens to you, I will feel responsible."

"Why?" I was genuinely surprised.

"Because…I care about you and…your well-being."

"Why?" I asked again.

"Don't pretend you are stupid," he seemed frustrated. "You've had so many narrow escapes through actually BEING stupid. Even your sister Abigail doesn't really believe that you have nine lives, although we joke about it. You've used at least five if you have! Julianna, this is me getting angry with you. I'm deadly serious."

But we dissolved into giggles and tears of laughter blinded me even as he said it.

"No, really. I do mean it. Tell me, please," he insisted and I saw the urgency in his face. I tried to read the eyes – there was something, but then it was gone.

"OK." I took a breath and spoke quickly. "In short, I woke up this morning in a dingy attic, unable to remember how I got there and with blood on my head from being bashed. When I eventually got out, through the window as you quite rightly deduced, I was chased by two hellhounds and ended up in Jack-The-Ripper alley. Whereupon I hailed a cab, went home and noticed that someone had shot me with enough drugs to put Keith Richards to sleep." I exhaled. "So, Medi, whatever it is, what does it do?"

"Midazolam," he answered patiently. "It's a sedative used for surgery, by dentists, and for treating epilepsy. It can cause short term memory loss. Likely you'll remember some things later. So, do you not remember anything? Were you attacked or assaulted?"

"No. I don't think that's what it was about. Checked a bit, seems OK but when I woke up my whole body felt a bit rough."

"It would do. Come on Jules! Think!"

"That's what I do best," I protested. "OK, this is what I can see in my head."

"Oh, bloody hell." He put his head in his hands.

"What? Can I finish?"

"Go on."

"No, really, what?"

He gave me the world-weary look, I knew this one. It was the one that said he knew all about the freaky things in my head, only too well.

"Kidnapped by aliens? Did they come to take you home?"

But I didn't smile. Now it was I, who was serious and more than a little fearful for the first time. I suddenly felt overwhelmed by a creeping dread. This was not over.

"OK," I went on with my eyes shut. "I keep getting flashbacks of a bar, coloured lights and lots of noise, you know music, gabble and then a fair-haired man, and a blond woman. She's tall. I know her. For some reason, I'm following them. They argued and left. She didn't protest or look forced. I didn't recognise him but somehow I feel I know him or he knows me."

"Was it a patient? Were you tailing a patient?" He pressed me for an answer.

"I don't know." I replied. I was a clinical psychologist and K knew I often had some rather interesting clients. But surely I wouldn't follow one of them?

K sighed. He told me that this sounded serious and that I probably couldn't ignore being probably kidnapped. I considered. "But I can't go to the police or anyone. You know how I feel about authorities." I shuddered, thinking about some bad experiences I'd had with people in authority in the past. "They don't get it right, I'm usually hated and also, what if I've done something illegal? I need to know more first."

"OK, well, it's likely that you might recover some memory in the next 24 hours. At least you might remember how you know the woman. And don't drink," he warned me.

Back at home, and never one to heed a warning, I headed for the whiskey bottle. I knocked back a large measure. Then, concerned that I might never recover the memory of the previous night, I decided to clean myself up in the shower and then lie down for a bit. Usually, sleep is not my most willing companion but, on this occasion, it came swiftly. Whether it was the trauma of the night's events or the effect of the alcohol, which had not been an inconsiderable portion, I began to dream.

Here, in the dream, strange sounds and images from far away begin to form like a running recording. The bar is too full, too noisy, the television of old at closedown, snow and fuzz. The sensation becomes a physical pain and, in this twilight, half-world, I cannot release the words to free the feeling. I'm imprisoned in my own mind. I can see the woman across the bar, she looks in my direction and instantly I know her. She's mouthing something at me and gesturing but I cannot hear and, in this world, I am frozen and mute. I glimpse myself in the mirror behind the bar. My hair is short, straight and light auburn. This is not me. The image warps and distorts as I drown in my own real face and the black curls of my real hair frond around my face. The woman fades. A snap-shot of a conversation, months back, an echoing voice, "Please help me, I'm afraid I will die. I'm not imagining this."

My eyes snapped open as I was sucked rapidly out of the vortex of the dream world. Lisa Warne! Of course! I made the connection the instant I jolted into consciousness but what had actually awakened me was a sound; my text alert.

I sluggishly dragged my aching body over to retrieve the text. When I read it, my insides contracted.

SEE U V SOON.

Alongside the words was a little emoticon blowing a heart-shaped kiss. I took a screenshot. But wait. The text alert wasn't my usual one. Someone had put it there, personalised it, someone who knew exactly who I was. I speed dialled K.

"K. K, I know who the woman was and why I was there. I need you to come around. Now!"

K arrived shortly after I called, collar turned up and dripping wet from sudden rainfall. He made for the kitchen and put the kettle on, knowing he wouldn't automatically be offered.

"I am improving, you know," I lied, "I was going to offer."

"Didn't want to leave it to chance." He smiled wryly. "So…I am working you know. We don't all have the luxury to pick and choose at our whim."

"OK." I began to relate the tale. "The woman is an ex-client, a patient. Her name is Lisa Warne. She first came to me four years ago."

I had just started practising psychology independently at the time I first met her. I had left my previous employment suddenly, after a difference of opinion and a mutual agreement to part 'amicably'. I'd found my niche working for myself, after many years of ups and downs with various employers who never seemed to do things properly. I'd often asked K, how he could stand it, working for the same employer for so many years and I marvelled at the way he had done so without incident. But K was pragmatic about such things.

"Just keep your head down, do your job well, take no shit, be liked." And K was infinitely likeable. He took no nonsense though. Years back, hot-headedness was his weakness but he'd mellowed into quiet assertiveness. K had a way I'd never have and will never understand. He'd removed me, on occasion physically, more times than I care to admit, from getting into a fight after an interaction with another human.

I continued with my tale to K, recalling that Lisa Warne was obviously a woman clinging to youth. Fit and gym-honed, tall, blond, sharp-featured but masking a hopeless vulnerability when it came to members of the opposite gender. Not that I could talk. In my work, I can read people with almost magical acuity of mind but in personal relationships, I have no clue. Lisa had been in an abusive relationship with somebody else's husband who presumably was similarly abusing the wife. It was the worst kind of abuse; a slow drip, drip of psychological discombobulation until the person who existed originally was no longer there. She needed to talk and I listened.

"In the end," Lisa told me, "I just had to break away." She had initially believed his marriage was over and had continued, naively, to believe that the wife and her lover were living apart. When the wife had finally had enough, Lisa too abandoned her lover. It happened by chance, as it so often does. Lisa had received a text from her boyfriend's wife. Lisa realised that he had been lying to them both for four years.

"I wrote to her," she said, "and I told her that he had been fooling us both. I really believed that he was going to marry me and we could have a life together." She had looked up at me with wide eyes, as if she thought I would not believe her. "I know now that my life would have been hell as he was the oddest and perhaps cruellest person I have ever met. But that's also what was weirdly attractive about him too. He made you feel that he'd specially selected you above all the other ordinary ones. In my eyes, his wife was much more beautiful than me and he always told me she was much better too. Why would you put up with that? But it was like being under some sort of spell. Does that make sense?"

"It makes perfect sense to me," I had replied, thinking of my own struggles at times.

She went on, "What was so disconcerting was that when I did finally communicate with his wife, she said a very similar thing. When I did find out, I knew that his wife was going to divorce him and I was determined to leave him too."

But by then, he had drawn her into his web of deceit too far to allow her to escape easily. With fingers in many pies, what he had revealed to her had ensnared her too deeply to simply walk away. When he could no longer control his ex-wife, he turned his full attention to my client and she was not strong enough to resist.

The man in question, Marcus Elliot, had owned a string of businesses, the most successful of which was a nightclub called 'Smiths'. He had, amongst embezzlement and tax fraud, been involved with several young women who were unfortunate enough to cross his path. Elliot had a reputation for the sordid. Girlfriends were trophies and never respected. Even in his early working career, he'd been accused of sexual harassment. Being hauled into the manager's office had no impact on him; it simply increased his arrogance. The women did not persevere with any complaints, so he got away with it.

He became infamous when a party ended spectacularly when a young woman, little more than a child, plummeted to her death from the rooftop of his club. Elliot's involvement was very suspicious, some suggested that he pushed her, others that he drove her to suicide. But those who served him slavishly, in his pay or thrall, managed to cover it up, despite the press reports about the 'young girl's rooftop dive of death' and he avoided the ensuing scandal.

Lisa knew all about his involvement with this incident and that his club was little more than a front for trafficking cocaine, heroin, vice-girls and more. She had more knowledge than his ex-wife, who thankfully, cut ties virtually unscathed. But Lisa was a different personality-type. Heavily involved in many of his wrongdoings and weak of character, she suffered abuse until she was broken but trapped.

When she came to me, Lisa Warne feared for her life at the hands of Marcus Elliot or one of his minions. I am ashamed to say that, at first, I believed her tale to be a fantastic hyperbole. As time went on, however, I knew she was telling the truth and as she begged me to help her, I found myself irresistibly drawn to the task, perilous though I knew it would be. My twin, Abigail, warned me extensively about becoming too involved.

"All your life, Julianna, you have been drawn to the bizarre and dangerous. Your thrill-seeking nonsense will be the death of you one day. Please, don't get involved in this. Do you remember how much pain you caused yourself last time you allowed someone to get under your skin?"

I did. Only too well. My arms and thighs still bear the scars. If I close my eyes now, I can still feel the hot sting of the razor as I drew it across my limbs, desperate to feel something tangible, any emotion instead of the numb muteness I suffered. My mirror lay in pieces, shattered as I had hammered my head against it, trying to eradicate the image of the person I could not recognise and identify as my own. But I held the fears at bay, willpower had boxed it up and put it away marked 'do not open'.

"You are different to most people," Abigail had continued, "If you take on too much of others' pain, you will suffer. I cannot rescue you again and again. Find yourself something ordinary! Marry! Listen to K. But do not carry on down this path of destruction. Already there has been immeasurable loss. Be a little more like me. Marry well, live well. I may not seem to be entirely fulfilled but I have a degree of happiness, whatever that means."

Did I listen? Of course not. Although twins, Abigail and I could not have been more different. I was intrigued by this woman and her story. I was also intrigued by her former lover. Never had I encountered such a vivid description of character so devoid of humanity, with the ability to feel no remorse or human compassion. By the time I had a few sessions with Lisa, I felt I knew him as well as she did.

The last time Lisa came to me she was very agitated and seemed to have peaked in her desperation.

"Please, do you think you can meet me tomorrow night in the bar of Smiths? I'm supposed to meet him there and pose as his girlfriend while he strikes one of his deals. The thing is there's no telling what he'll want me to do. He's just as likely to try and set me up as a little gift to one of the men as part of the deal being sealed. I can't refuse; I can't tell you how many times this has happened before. Well, you know some of it. It keeps them 'sweet' he says. He truly doesn't see anything wrong with it. He punishes me if I don't go along with it."

"But you are not with him now, are you?" I raised an eyebrow. "You don't have to do this."

"I don't know," she looked down at her hands. "I just can't help but go along with it. It doesn't matter how many times I rehearse it in my head, it is different when he's there in front of me. I can't explain."

I started to speak again.

"You'd have to meet him," she interrupted, "then you'd understand."

"Believe me, there is nothing that would fascinate me more." I replied.

"Then meet me tomorrow and you may get your wish."

I knew then that I would meet her.

The plan did not take long to formulate. As a precaution, because of what I had been told about this character, I chose to adopt a disguise. Alas, it was too late when I realised that no disguise would ever aid me. He already knew who I was and where I would be.

The evening arrived. My greatest mistake was not telling K. I didn't know quite what to expect but as I warily entered the bar alone, it met most of my preconceptions about tackiness and depravity.

Music beat loudly as coloured lights strobed in time with it. In the middle, a nearly naked vixen snaked around a pole, thrusting her crotch towards leering males as they deftly inserted ample wads of cash into her jewel-encrusted thong. Her face bore the expression of well-practised lust but her eyes were impassive as I concluded she must be nearing the end of her shift.

I moved purposefully to the bar, expertly elbowing my way to the front and ordered a Jack Daniels and Coke. I was acutely aware of the male-heavy environment and that several eyes were upon me. I was used to this sort of attention but remained forever mystified about the interest I seemed to create in others. I always joked that I must exude an invisible scent that drew people in. It certainly wasn't something I craved deliberately or consciously but sometimes I used it to my advantage, as noted often and with a certain distaste by Abigail.

I had sat on a barstool, eyeing my unrecognisable self in the mirror and trying to avoid eye contact with people around me. I wanted to be completely focused on the task at hand. I spotted Lisa entering with four men, one of whom I presumed must be Elliot. From the way she had talked about him, it could only be him. He was not tall but walked with enough swagger to suggest importance or at least an inflated ego. He had the sharp suit and blond tanned look to carry it off superficially and his attention to detail suggested precision, obsessiveness and vanity. His nails were more beautifully manicured than any woman's I had seen recently and his cufflinks and watches were expensive and designer brand. In fact, only a quick appraisal of the watch suggested a rare, limited-edition timepiece. This man meant to impress and a somewhat vulgar showiness emanated from his entire being. It wasn't natural though, it was carefully studied and it suggested a background that was very different from the one he was trying to project. However, those with an untrained eye would no doubt see what he wanted them to.

I watched them speaking for a while. I was well-practised at people-watching and could do so relatively undetected. They sipped drinks and talked. Then he made some sort of hand gesture and the other men left. This was when things became heated between Elliot and Lisa. He was obviously very angry and tried aggressively to grab her by the arm. She flinched and pushed him away, obviously trying to leave but he had held her fast. They had both left; she a little under protest but not markedly so to any casual observers. This was the moment I decided to follow them.

When I was on the other side of the exit door, I stood under the fluorescent lights which hummed and flickered intermittently. There was no sign of Lisa and Elliot. Without warning, a hand reached out from behind and clapped itself over my mouth. Another pair of rough arms held mine fast behind my back and as I tried to struggle, a short, sharp jab into the neck ensured my swift descent into unconsciousness.

I must have woken just once, as I was vaguely aware of lights swishing past overhead, dim voices and then a sense of panic and a sharp crack on the back of the head. After that, nothing. The next thing I remember is, of course, waking up in the dingy room.

All of this was the memory I related to K as he stood there, listening intently, never having broken my tale to sip his now-cold tea.

"So, I think it's time to finally go to the police," he said at last, "not only have you been kidnapped and assaulted but it looks like a possible attempted murder and a missing person as well."

"I know!" I agreed. "Someone really didn't want me to find out what was going on! But we have to be careful. Lisa could be in more danger now, if she isn't already dead."

"But you have to involve the police now!" he cried. Then, in sudden realisation he wailed, "Oh my god! You want to find out what Elliot has been up to first!"

"I do want to know," I admitted, "but I will go to the police to get them on to it because Lisa is now missing and I have vital information. One of my university friends is a D.I. now. Charlotte Pierrepoint. I like her and she's sensible."

"Julianna. You need to go to them. Look, why don't we eat something and get it all straight."

"OK. That would help." I suddenly felt faint.

"How long is it since you had something to eat?" he eyed me suspiciously.

"Yesterday? I don't know. All right, I'll go with you and we can talk it through."

The restaurant, our favourite, was much busier than usual. I was used to it being a tranquil space where I could relax and enjoy some beautifully presented offerings. As soon as we entered, I remembered how long it was since we had been there. I glanced at my reflection in the mirror behind the table. Once again, I felt displaced, as if I couldn't quite recognise myself. My sense of identity has never been strong and often the person in the mirror is hard to reconcile with the body my mind inhabits. I looked pale and slightly emaciated in the face, cheekbones sharper than usual, dark circles under green eyes with pinpoint pupils, dark wavy hair curling around the hollow cheeks. I sat down abruptly.

As we chatted about what to do next, or rather skirted delicately around the issue, the noise in the background intensified until K's mouth moved but I could no longer understand the words. I receded into the walls as the incessant background chatter punctuated by the occasional screaming whoop of joy from the middle table, beat to the terrifying rhythm of the clock on the wall, growing ever more insistent. Almost overwhelmed by the rising panic that possessed me, I tried to choke it back down as I fumbled blindly for my possessions and lurched wildly towards the nearest exit.

I was aware of K in the background calling me but I paid no heed to that as his call seemed to come from another, distant world. When I finally reached the outside, the consuming urge was to run and scream and never stop. But I stayed, propping myself up against the wall as the full force of the fear erupted and I buckled, shaking uncontrollably, hyperventilating, unable to control it, exploding into white light.

Thus, K found me and grounded me, talking to me in a soothing voice.

"I don't understand it," I muttered.

"I've been expecting this," he replied, "It's natural after the events. Go to the police, report her missing at least and tell them what happened to you."

The mobile in my pocket rang out. K fished for it and upon retrieving it, answered.

"Abigail," answered K. "Impeccable timing!"

"Kiaron? Where's Julianna? Why are you answering her phone? Is she all right?" demanded Abigail.

"Yes, yes. It's fine. All under control."

"Oh, I see. No, I don't see." I could hear her voice clearly.

"Give that to me!" I yelled with impatience. "Abigail. Stop talking about me and talk to me."

"I just wondered if you'd actually done anything sensible like going to the police yet. Or maybe you are avoiding the situation you seem to have landed in altogether?" barked Abigail.

"We're on our way to see Charlotte in fact," I said. And I hung up. "Why do I suddenly feel like a little kid? And you are no help!" I shouted petulantly at K. "I swear you talk about me when I'm not there!"

K knew that this was the adrenalin talking, that it was only an overload of chemicals signalling my neurotransmitters to fight or flee. But I knew from his face, which even to me was transparent, that my words had stung.

Still trembling slightly, I felt around awkwardly in my pockets until my hand alighted on the prize it sought. I lit up and turned my head to one side so that my smoke-shrouded profile shut him out. It wasn't that I didn't want to say something, I really did. But it remained stuck. Inside my head, voices screamed at me but I could not bring the words to my mouth. I would never spill my feelings. The mobile ringing, however, had reminded me the text message. There was somebody, probably Elliot, who knew who I was and was definitely coming after me.

I thought about it long after I should have been asleep and as I drifted off, my night was plagued by unrepentant visions of Lisa's face swimming in and out of focus, the room where I was held captive and shadowy, whispering voices closing in from behind, so close I could feel their breath on my neck. In one distorted dream, I had lost my way, was searching for my car. I met Lisa on a path, lit by the dim street lamp and I warned her to turn back or at least stay where it was well-lit. There was a choice of two paths ahead of me, I could take the lower route to the car park past the playground or I could take the upper path into the forest. I wanted to travel along the lower path, afraid as I was, inexplicably, of the creaking swing on the children's play area. I knew this was the shortest and obvious route to take but somehow, I ended up on the upper path and facing the trees. From the darkness came the two snarling, fang bearing hounds that I had encountered in the backyard of the attic room, my erstwhile prison. I waved my phone torch at them and they ran off. In my dream though, this brought little relief, as I knew I still had to negotiate the strangely sinister playground. I almost tiptoed past, all the time sensing that something was still lurking out there, ready to spring upon me. I could not find my car so I somehow found myself in that strange leap of time so often encountered in dreams, I was inside a stranger's car and hotwiring it to drive to safety. The dream culminated in diving from the driver's seat just in time to see the car plunging from a clifftop as I rolled to safety. I woke up, bathed in sweat, although I did wonder what I might have made of that dream if a client had related it to me. I also wondered what Abi and K would make of it and decided to keep it to myself.

The next morning, still vaguely disquieted, I went to my office as usual. When I had spoken to her, Charlotte had listened to my tale intently and during the revelation, a stocky and friendly-faced man had entered the room.

"Julianna, this is my sergeant, Joe Turner. He needs to hear this too," Charlotte had said in a very formal tone.

Joe Turner had eyed me carefully. His face was open and honest and I liked him immediately. Evidently, he liked me too as his eyes wore the expression of an adoring puppy dog. The look was not reserved for me alone though, Charlotte received the same attention, although perhaps with a little more professional caution. I smiled slightly but continued the tale, ending with the unresolved text message.

Back in my office, it was, to all intents and purposes, an ordinary day without incident, but I felt far from ordinary. My visit to the police had yielded little comfort; they were on standby and had filed a 'missing person' report for Lisa but for myself, there were only reprimands for not contacting them earlier and nothing substantial enough to offer me any protection as wished for by the concerned K. I buzzed the next client in.

I had my back to the door when it swung slowly open after a tentative cursory knock. As I turned, I met her eyes and was surprised and delighted, albeit a little unnerved. Something wasn't right.

"Lisa!" I exclaimed. "You're OK!"

"I'm sorry, Julianna, so sorry."

"But why are you sorry? I'm so glad you are…" I didn't even get to finish my sentence because right then Marcus

Elliot stepped out of the shadow of the door, closing it silently behind him.

"I take it you haven't come for a therapy session?" I suggested bravely.

The voice that replied was chilling; it was grating and gravelly and salaciously hissing all at once. It was like no other I had encountered before and I truly felt as if I was in the presence of something dark and unfathomable. My skin crawled in his presence and he exuded magnetic repulsion. Yet I was transfixed. I felt as if I already knew him, even as if I might have encountered him in another life, another time or even in the dark well of my own self.

In a moment, the two of them were upon me though and I smelled and tasted the heady metallic sensation of a narcotic flooding my system and carrying me into darkness.

Once again, I found myself half-waking in unfamiliar surroundings. This time, though, I knew who had brought me here and I could just make out the shadowy figure of a man silhouetted against the covered window.

"You may think you are clever," he hissed. "You may think you are going to have me put away for what you know about me. Don't imagine you are going to save Lisa. She has helped me now but she's the walking dead. And actually, sweetie, it's pretty much your fault. I know what she has told you but no one ever leaves me without a price to pay."

I felt sickened. "Are you going to try to kill me? It won't help you. You are right, I do know a lot about you but do you think I would keep it to myself?" I was thinking quickly, trying to outpace my captor.

In the dim light, I could picture his smirk as he answered me. "Yes. I do think you would keep it to yourself. I think that because I know you would want all the glory of handing me over. And you want to know some answers. It makes you feel good to rescue someone, you think it vindicates you. I know this because I can get inside your mind. I'm the bad thoughts inside your head. You're so EASY to read. No. I'm not going to kill you right now, right here. But you will be dead anyway. Inside you will be dead and you will do anything to actually be dead. And you know what I'm talking about, don't you? It's written all over you. I can smell it."

Something I hadn't really felt for a while began to lurch up from deep inside me. I'd like to call it fear but it was more than that, it was an all-encompassing sensation, not sickness, what was it? It was as if I knew that I could die or that I could lose something so important to me that I would never recover. I didn't fear death, I feared maiming; I feared the loss of my important people and that was what crept over me in waves now. This reptilian creature had the power to take so much. We met eye-to-eye and I saw the dark side of the looking glass.

"See, I know all about you," he said, licking his lips salaciously, "and I have had you marked for a very long time."

"Why?" I slurred at him. "I don't even know you; I've read about you but…" My voice trailed off because I was finding it so hard to concentrate.

"I hate you," he said simply, "and I am going to destroy you."

"For Lisa telling me things?"

"Much, much more than that. I knew you long before that. But first, enjoy these sensations."

He turned on a projector; a hand-held-style flickering film. As I watched the images unfold, I felt the icy-cold chill re-entering my veins. And I floated just above normality.

I'm drowning. All around me the water is closing in like a crystal-black bubble. I am engulfed in negativity. I am drowning. Why can't I outrun my brain, leave my mind? I'm immersed in a spiral so black and deep-set, I cannot survive it. I am going to die, slowly, painfully, a metaphorical dance through my own consciousness en-route to my own destruction. The film he was showing me was torturous to my mind; it told a kind of story in abstract, surreal nightmare-like imagery. I recognised some of the plot but the cocktail of drugs he was administering merged with the screen images so that the visuals took shape and began to crawl from the screen and rise up in terrifying shapes surrounding me in the room. I could not distinguish between the voices in my head and those on screen; I could not differentiate between the flickering and distorted assortment of characters on screen or those that seemed to appear beside me and brush my face with their fingers. It was the perfect form of torture as my demons and terrors awakened and shook hands with my present. This elaborate piece of art had been designed exclusively for me, for my perceived part in events I only half understood but which crossed paths with my own long-buried history. What I knew about him through Lisa was only part of the reason I was here. He had a need to protect his reputation for sure but that she had landed in my office was a coincidence he had exploited. I had been a marked target long before and finally, the journey was complete. His persecution was personal as he kept me teetering on the edge of death's abyss.

Drifting in and out of consciousness and unable to escape from the unfolding and sickening nightmare, the living corpses of bloody adult-sized foetuses seemed to crawl out of the screen and over my body. Circling and surrounding me, they pointed their unformed fingers at me and jabbed at my eyes with these thin and nail-less appendages. A laughing girl distorted into a grey and melting shadow as her handsome beaux tore off his mask, revealing a skinless red skull with empty sockets who sucked the breath from her lungs, even as my breath began to leave mine. From somewhere beyond the screen, I saw a shadowy figure depart and in the depths of my addled and terrified mind, I knew that he would return with further and more physical tortures. I tried to cry out but no sound would come out and I could not make sense of my thoughts.

It happened quite suddenly, just as I was finally slipping from consciousness and descending with merciful release into the blackness from which I hoped I would not wake, I was yanked roughly from my restraints. Hardly knowing what was happening, I collapsed forward groggily and felt myself being dragged painfully across the floor. In dread, I anticipated Elliot's further torture and truly believed I would be maimed or killed. I tried to get up but the drugs in my system prevented me from moving. I tried to bring my vision into focus gasping lungfuls of air as the hallucinatory distortions still plagued my confused brain.

Dimly, I noticed the hands that had released me and which were now dragging me felt smaller than those belonging to a man.

"Get up! Get out!" she hissed and I felt the shocking splash of water soaking my face. "I will try to keep him occupied. I'm sorry; I had no choice, please!"

Again, icy water hit me in the face and soaked my limbs. The sudden cold revived me a little and I began to crawl towards what I thought was a door.

With effort, I managed to hook my hand underneath it. I pulled and miraculously, it opened, revealing grey stone walls and concrete stairs spiralling up and down. I heaved my body along the floor and through the opening. But as I did so, I was aware of the sound of a scuffle and shouting.

I looked up and down in the bland, beige corridor I had entered. There were metallic stairs like a fire exit, winding up and down and dim, faulty strip lighting above. I crouched in the stairwell and I could just make out the shadows of a man and woman struggling and the woman, Lisa, screaming as he rained blows down upon her face. I cowered in the shadows as they burst through the exit, the door thrust open wide now and I heard the clanking on the stairs above me as she seemed to escape then be caught; the scuffling and dragging noises seemed to continue up several flights of stairs but I could do nothing until the feeling in my limbs returned enough for me to stand. I whimpered in frustration, knowing that she would surely meet her death and that he would come back for me.

It seemed like a lifetime but it was probably only a matter of minutes when I tried again frantically to stand. If I could get away…if I could save her…I heaved myself up and I could still hear the screaming and clattering on the stairs; the heavy bang of a metal door above. I moved up the stairs, unthinkingly, with no plan in my mind but with the urgency of the situation driving me on. I reached the door I had heard and with all my strength, I yanked at the metal bar across it and it came away, providing me with at least some sort of weapon as I charged through.

As I rounded the corner on the rooftop, I saw them struggling. All the time my heart was beating a rhythm *Too late, not yet, too late, not yet.*

We locked eyes and he grinned at me like a demon.

I shouted once and then they were gone, both of them, over the edge.

I was stunned for a second, and then I was livid!

"No!" I yelled and ran to the edge. Behind me, the clanging of urgent, heavy footsteps sounded as the police charged up the stairwell.

"Too bloody late!" I rounded on them viciously. "We failed! I failed." Then I looked over the precipice for the inevitable. There it was, the crumpled and twisted heap on the pavement below, a red stain spreading out around her.

Then a dreadful realisation dawned on me. There was only one body. Hers.

Already the crowd was gathering below, cordoned off and controlled by the police presence on the ground. The ones on the roof were making their way down. Only Catherine and K remained briefly and K took me by the hand and led me down to make our statements.

When I entered the house later that evening, I longed for the silence. But my place of sanctuary offered me no solace tonight. Old sensations needled me with insistent fingers, feelings insidiously infiltrating my place of safety. I leaned against the front door and took a deep breath.

I fought it so hard but I could not shake it off. The familiar prickle of anticipation had me reaching for the pills and a huge slug of Jack Daniel's almost without thinking. Today, when failure stalked me like a spectre, I waited for this safety net to engulf me with softness and warmth, the way nothing else could.

Later, Abi was at the door with K.

"Oh no, Julianna." She only had to look at my eyes to realise what I had done. "Surely, those problems are all in the past now? That time…it's history…you have to move on."

"Not really in the mood right now, OK?" I said.

"No. I can tell. Let me know if you need me." But she was downcast as she left. She was concerned and I felt guilty for it. K stayed and he smiled. "She's genuinely worried about you. I am too. Please don't start using those pills and drinking again."

"You can trust me, I promise," I lied. "I just needed to be calm and I have a terrible headache. It's a bad day."

It was definitely a bad day. With several questions unanswered. How had Elliot got away? How did he know anything about me? Why had he come after me? It was personal and I didn't know why. And a woman had died.

"You did your best, Julianna. It really wasn't your fault," said K looking at me kindly.

I locked eyes with him and in that moment I knew what I was doing and I knew I only did it to divert him, but I still kissed him on the mouth.

He definitely kissed me back.

With my eyes closed, my mind raced with the unanswered questions, and in the midst of it all, I wondered, if maybe this could work. But even then, the face of Marcus Elliot loomed up in my mind and I knew that I hadn't seen the last of him.